The Enlistment:
A Frankie Blaine Story

The Enlistment:
A Frankie Blaine Story

Janet R Stafford

Squeaking Pips Press, Inc.
2017

First Printing: 2017

ISBN 978-0-9992285-0-0

Squeaking Pips Press, Inc.
Hillsborough, NJ 08844

www.squeakingpips.com

Ordering Information:

Special discounts are available on quantity purchases by associa-
tions, educators, and others.

For details, contact jstafford@squeakingpipsinc.com.

Dedication

To Kristina Bush Shebchuk,
who loves Frankie Blaine.

Contents

Acknowledgements

Thank you to all those who have pushed, encouraged, and stood by me during an amazing journey that began with a single book.

Special thanks go to my beta readers and cheerleaders: Kristina Shebchuk, Dan Bush, Laura Wimbrow, Laurie Doscher, and Carol Drews.

Preface

I am a history geek. I don't know when it started, but I always wondered what it was to live in another time or place. I'm also kind of a religion geek. Don't let this scare you. I'm a nice person who happens to have a Master of Divinity degree and who, although not ordained, has served six United Methodist churches as an assistant minister, educator, youth director, communications director and probably a few other unlisted things. That's a lot of hats to wear, but they keep me busy.

I also have a Ph.D. in North American Religion and Culture. I enjoyed the classes I took about the nineteenth century most, one of which was a tutorial that dealt with scandals in the ministry. For the required research paper, I found a sad, tragic story about a talented, charismatic young minister in Warren County, NJ named Jacob Harden. When Harden ended up in a shotgun marriage, his response to it was... well, shall we say it did not live up to the expectations one might have of a clergyman?

For some reason, the story stuck with me and I wondered how one would fictionalize it. A few years after my Ph.D. was granted, I decided to try writing the story as a novel.

The end product was a character-driven tale set in 1860-61 called SAINT MAGGIE. The story is about a good-hearted, Methodist widow named Maggie who runs a boarding house and receives the new minister, Jeremiah Madison, as a new boarder. The cast of characters in Maggie's house is eclectic: a failed writer named Chester Carson; Jim "Grandpa" O'Reilly (an old indigent Irishman); a struggling young lawyer by the name of Edgar Lape; and the undertaker's apprentice (Patrick McCoy). I gave Maggie two teenage daughters: Lydia, the sensible one who has a knack for nursing, and her younger sister Frances (known as Frankie), the outspoken, opinionated one. Completing the cast are Emily and Nate Johnson. Emily is Maggie's closest friend and the boarding house cook. Nate is a carpenter. The Johnsons are Black, which does not sit well with the town folk because they live in Maggie's house on the town square. Finally, we have Elijah Smith, the editor of a penny weekly called the *Gazette*. A former Quaker and self-proclaimed free-thinker, Eli is sweet on Maggie and we are introduced to their romance and eventual marriage in the first few chapters of the novel.

I became a self-published author in 2011 and released my work through my micro-publishing company, Squeaking Pips Press, Inc.

I actually thought SAINT MAGGIE would be a single novel and that I would move on to other stories. It is funny how one little question can change things. While speaking about SAINT MAGGIE at book clubs and other groups, people repeatedly asked: "What happens next?" As it turned out, readers loved the characters and wanted more stories about them.

And that's how I ended up writing a series comprised of novels, short stories, and now a novella about Maggie, her family, and friends.

This novella is the first Saint Maggie "spin off." Its central character is Maggie's daughter Frankie. Other stories and novels about Frankie and her sister Lydia are in the offing.

Let me conclude by noting that life is funny. I would never have thought that a solitary research paper would lead me to write a series of novels and stories.

Introduction

As explained in the Preface, Frankie Blaine is the youngest daughter of boarding house owner Maggie Blaine Smith. Frankie made her appearance in SAINT MAGGIE at the tender age of fourteen. Aside from Maggie's brief journal entry at the story's opening, Frankie is the first character to utter a line. That line is "I hate corsets and crinolines!" It lets us know immediately that she is a handful.

Frankie is outspoken, stubborn, intelligent, compassionate, and somewhat impulsive. THE ENLISTMENT centers on what happens to her when her beau, Patrick McCoy, enlists in the army. It is 1862. The Civil War is raging, and Frankie is feeling frustrated and helpless. She is afraid Patrick will be injured or, worse yet, killed. And she rebels when she is repeatedly told that she must stay at home and sedately roll bandages and scrape the lint from clothing to be used by army doctors to pack wounds. Frankie knows she can do more, perhaps even something great. But what?

And so off we go on an adventure with a young woman trying to find her way in a society that insists women stay within their "sphere," even in the midst of a terrible war.

The list below provides information regarding THE ENLISTMENT's chronological place (as of summer 2017) among the other stories in the Saint Maggie universe.

"The Dundee Cake" (short story)	1852
SAINT MAGGIE (novel)	1860-61
THE ENLISTMENT (novella)	1862
WALK BY FAITH (novel)	1863
"The Christmas Eve Visitor" (short story)	1863
A TIME TO HEAL (novel)	1863
SEEING THE ELEPHANT (novel)	1864

The Enlistment

Frances "Frankie" Blaine didn't know exactly when she had fallen in love with Patrick McCoy. They had been friends for a long time. He had come to live at her mother's boarding house after taking a job as the undertaker's apprentice. That was in the summer of 1859. Later a shocking series of events in 1860-61 shook the Blaine household and the little town of Blaineton, New Jersey. It was Patrick's interest in medicine and science that helped answer a crucial question, making a favorable impression on Frankie.

As the town and the boarding house recovered, a feeling began to grow between the two young people. And then one day he took her hand. It was in April of 1861. Patrick was eighteen years old, but Frankie would not be fifteen until June. It didn't matter. They both knew something was happening.

Slowly Frankie came to the realization that she was in love with Patrick. Everything was full of hope, until that evening in early August of 1862 when Patrick told her something that made her gasp.

"What? Oh, Patrick! Why?"

He had just told her that he was going to enlist in the Army.

Patrick took a deep breath and thought: *Here we go.* This girl could be a handful – and yet that was one of the reasons he loved her. Frankie brimmed with life and she had a mind of her own.

The two were sitting on the porch steps. The sun had just begun to set. It was the time of day that Mr. Borden, the town's Lamplighter, went down the street. Frankie and Patrick watched as he paused by the gas lamp in front of the Second Street Boarding House, lifted the pole, and lit the lamp.

When Mr. Borden smiled in their direction, the two waved at him. Once he had moved on, Frankie said, "I don't want you to go, Pat."

"Yeah, well," he muttered, averting his eyes, "we have to win this war. I have a duty, you know."

She bristled. "A duty? To do what? Die?"

The war had been going on between the states for a year and four months, and during that time Frankie had eagerly read her stepfather's newspaper, *The Gazette.* She had learned all about battles in far-flung places like Fort Sumter, Boonville, Lexington, Bull Run, Leesburg, Hampton Roads, Shiloh, Williamsburg, and Chattanooga.

So many names. So many places. So many battles. So many deaths.

Frankie had been worried when Patrick went off with his employer, Mr. Meany, to help him set up a business to embalm soldiers' bodies and send them home to grieving families. That had been in July of 1861.

The young couple had written to each other regularly and then, abruptly, in February of 1862, Patrick walked up the steps to the boarding house saying he had seen enough.

Ever since that time, he had taken over as the town's undertaker, a job that consisted mainly of building caskets and some other furniture, making arrangements for burial, and helping families lay loved ones out in the parlor for viewing prior to the funeral service. He seldom embalmed anyone. The process was expensive and wasn't needed since bodies normally were laid out on a cooling board.*

But now Patrick, the boy she loved with all her heart and who had come home disgusted at the destruc-

---

* The star indicates that the word can be found in the Glossary at the end of the book.

4

tion and loss of life he had seen, was saying he wanted to join the army.

On one hand, Frankie was afraid for him. He could get wounded or, worse yet, killed. On the other, she felt oddly jealous. It was as if he was abandoning her again to go on an adventure, an adventure in which she could not participate. Patrick would be serving his country in a way that was denied to her.

Frankie never could understand why boys and men were afforded a wide range of opportunities while those available to women and girls were greatly limited. She knew all about the "sphere of men" – the rough but exciting world of politics, business, and war – and the "sphere of women" – the softer realm of religion, home, and family. And yet Frankie was well aware that women were every bit as resourceful, tough, and intelligent as men. It was no wonder that the spirited young woman chafed at her role in society.

And now her beau was going to war and she was supposed to sit back and meekly accept it.

Unlike her pacifist stepfather, who as a former Quaker rejected violence and aggression, Frankie had mixed feelings about this war. She understood that it had become a vast killing machine, but she hated slavery as well as the fact that the Union had been broken in two. She also understood that there seemed to be no way for the United States of America and the Confederate States of America to come to terms. Although she did not like the idea that a conclusion would involve one nation's loss and the other one's triumph, it seemed necessary for both sides had given up completely on talk.

As the elfin redhead brooded on Patrick's an-nouncement, her young man was watching her. Every time his girl got cross, he could swear her eyes turned emerald green, and they were brilliant now, so she had to be furious. He finally said, "Look, Frankie, Edgar and I have been talking this over and –"

"Oh, I know you've been talking it over," she interrupted. "I've heard it at the supper table every night for months now." Frankie's eyes pooled with tears, making them all the brighter. "I thought you were back to stay. You said you'd had enough."

"I wasn't in the army then. You know that." Patrick was a fair-looking young man of nineteen, with a shock of hair the color of mahogany and eyes as blue as a deep sea. His long fingers laced together and then unlaced again. "But I have seen the worst that can happen to soldiers. I saw the bodies. I saw what a minié ball* and shrapnel can do to a man." He heaved a sigh. "Frankie, I was so disgusted with Mr. Meany. Embalming doesn't cost nearly as much as what he charged. He was cheating soldiers' families, taking advantage of their grief and their need to see loved ones one last time. He wasn't helping anyone but himself." He glanced at her. "That's why I decided to leave. I went with him because I thought I could do something, to make a difference, to help in some way. But once I saw what was going on I realized Mr. Meany was making money from people's pain."

Frankie brushed unruly strands of red hair back from her face. Her hair always managed to escape both braid and bun, which annoyed her to no end but for which she could find no cure. "Look, Pat, if you join the army, you'll have a gun in your hands. You'll be shooting at the Johnnies* and they'll be shooting at you. What difference could *you* possibly make besides losing your life and making us all sad, too?"

"I don't know. I *do* know this, though, we all thought this thing was going to be over in a few months, but now there's no end in sight. Frankie, I can't sit back anymore and let someone else do the fighting." It was impossible to look at her when she was this distressed, so Patrick focused on the square across the street as he

6

spoke. The parklike environs were filled now with dense summer greenery. Tree branches created a canopy of heavy leaves that during the day left dappled shade on the bushes and flower beds. Once upon a time, back in the town's early history, sheep used to graze on that patch of green.

As he gazed at the square Patrick suddenly realized that Frankie had no idea what things were like elsewhere. He had seen the devastation left by the war while working with Mr. Meany in Virginia and he still had nightmares about it. But Frankie, living in the safe little enclave of Blaineton, had no idea what was out there, other than what she read in the *Gazette*.

Across the square, as the sun set, the yellow glow of oil lamps began appearing in windows.

Patrick said, "You've got to understand, Frankie. I don't want to go. I want to stay here with you. But this is something I need to do. Edgar and I will be going down to Flemington to enlist at Camp Fair Oaks. If all goes well, they'll accept us, and we'll join the Fifteenth New Jersey Volunteers. I'm sorry, but that's the way it's got to be."

Frankie's lower lip trembled.

Patrick braced himself. She was about to cry. He hated it when she cried.

"Will you be back after you enlist?" she asked in a quavering little voice, which nearly broke his heart.

Steeling himself, he said, "No. I hear they'll send us right into training."

At this, she leaped to her feet. "Oh, Patrick! How could you?" And, gathering up her skirts, she bolted off the porch and into the boarding house, slamming the door behind her.

Patrick threw his head back and emitted a frustrated groan.

"The course of true love never did run smooth," a voice behind him said.

Patrick looked over his shoulder at Eli Smith, Frankie's stepfather. "That from the Bible?"

"Shakespeare. *A Midsummer Night's Dream.*" Using his cane, the portly man thumped over and eased himself down to sit on the step beside Patrick.

"I guess it doesn't matter if it's Shakespeare or the Bible. It's the truth," Patrick muttered. "Boy, is it ever true..."

"Yep." Eli's dark eyes peered out at the young man from behind wire rim eyeglasses. "So, tell me. What happened?"

"Told her I was going to Flemington tomorrow to enlist and that I wouldn't be coming back home. That made her angry."

"Ah."

Confused, Patrick turned to the middle-aged man. "What should I do, Eli?"

"Well, you're dealing with a woman, albeit a young one. Reactions vary from one to the next, but I'd say give her some time, and then go and tell her how much you care about her and how sorry you are that your news upset her."

Patrick frowned. "But –"

"*And,*" Eli continued, "tell her that you have a patriotic duty to perform and will try your level best to get home in one piece."

"Aw, she'll never accept that!"

"Fine. How about picking a nice bouquet of flowers and giving them to her?"

"That won't work, either, Eli. This is Frankie we're talking about, not her mother."

The older man laughed. "True. Mrs. Smith isn't quite that stubborn, and she does love flowers." He paused a moment. "However, allow me to say that my lovely bride is not at all happy that Carson and I plan to cover the war for the *Gazette* by following your Regiment. Once we get permission from the government, that is.

When she heard my news, Mrs. Smith said one word, 'Fine.' And then she walked away. Very quickly."

Patrick heaved a long sigh. "Edgar tells me Liddy is being stoic."

"Yep," Eli replied. "Lydia got the stoicism. Frankie got the excitability. They're sisters who are opposites in most ways."

"Why do you suppose women get so upset over us leaving?"

Eli glanced at the young man and smiled faintly. "Because they love us."

"Must be hard being a woman."

"Without a doubt."

Patrick stared out at Blaineton's darkening square. "Guess there aren't any easy decisions for any of us these days, huh?"

"With all due respect, my young friend, *most* decisions are not easy."

#

After running all the way to her bedroom on the second floor of the boarding house's "new wing," a weeping Frankie threw herself upon the bed.

Chloe Strong could hear the other girl's heart-rending sobs all the way down the hall. When Frankie had run through the kitchen, the concerned ten-year-old got up from the table where she had been reading a book and followed her friend.

Chloe and her mother, Matilda, arrived at the boarding house in early 1861. They had escaped from a plantation in Virginia, stumbled upon an Underground Railroad line*, and were smuggled north night after night by people of all kinds until they reached Blaineton.

As Chloe drew closer to Frankie's piteous sobs, she couldn't help but wonder what had happened. Sometimes the things her sixteen-year-old friend got upset over were confusing.

She stepped into the bedroom. "What's wrong?"

Frankie lifted her head and, eyes red-rimmed, stared at the girl with the black braids. "Patrick's going to join the army. He's enlisting tomorrow and won't be coming back."

Chloe walked to the bed and sat down beside her friend.

Frankie used the palm of her hand to wipe tears from her cheeks. "He could get killed. Oh, Chloe, what would I do if that happened?"

"I don't know. But we all lose people at one time or another and it's hard." After a couple seconds of silence, she murmured, "When they sold off my father and my brothers, I wanted to lay down and die."

The other girl sniffed and fumbled in her bodice* for a handkerchief.

Chloe looked earnestly into Frankie's watery eyes. "If I were you, I'd be proud Patrick's joining the army. If the rest of my family is still in Virginia and if the Union wins, we could be together again. That is," she added quietly, "if they're all still alive."

Touched, Frankie reached over and laid a hand on Chloe's arm. "I believe they are."

The younger girl offered up a brave smile.

Frankie took the moment of silence to blow her nose and then said, "You ever wish you could do something to help?"

Chloe nodded.

"Me too." After giving her nose one last swipe with the hankie, Frankie sighed. "I wish *I* could enlist."

"Girls can't be soldiers."

"No, I suppose not." Frankie sat up and brushed her hair back from her face. "But being a girl is so... inconvenient! I mean, why do we have to wear skirts? And those awful hoops and corsets!" She shuddered.

"Are they bad? I haven't worn hoops or a corset yet."

"They're both dreadful. With hoops, you have to be careful how you sit down or your skirts'll just fly up over your head and everyone'll be able to see your drawers.*"

Chloe laughed.

"And corsets!" Frankie rolled her eyes heavenward. "You get tied into them so tight you scarce can breathe. They're torture!" Getting control of herself, she sighed softly. "Oh, Chloe, there are so many things girls can't do. Have you ever thought about that?"

Chloe nodded. "Sure. And there're even more *colored* girls can't do."

Frankie frowned. "That's so unfair. Just because your skin is dark doesn't mean you're not clever. And just because we're both girls it doesn't mean we're not strong and that we can't fight."

"We fight every day just to get our voices heard."

"That's right! It's like trying to join the conversation at dinner time. I have to work hard just to get a word in edgewise." The redheaded young woman leaned toward her young friend. "You know, when I was your age, I used to play with a group of three boys – and I could best every one of them! Whatever they did, I did, too, and I did it better! I even got into fist fights, but I won those, too." She rested back against the bed's headboard. "They say women are the weaker sex, but I respectfully disagree."

"Me, too," Chloe opined. "My mommy is the strongest woman in the world, and she knows it. That's why she took the name 'Strong,' instead of the plantation master's name."

"And they say only men should fight," Frankie muttered. "Ha! I bet I could shoot a gun if I had to."

"I bet I could, too!" Chloe grinned. "Say, if we got hold of a gun we could go off to the woods and shoot at rocks and trees and things." She blew out a wistful breath. "I wish colored girls could enlist..."

"Wouldn't that be something," Frankie mused. "Both of us in the army..."

"We probably could win the war single-handed!"

"Bet we could! And you and I would be the heroines of the war."

The two collapsed into giggles. But once their laughter subsided, they fell into a reflective silence.

"Know what?" Chloe whispered.

"What?"

"I wish there wasn't a war."

Frankie nodded. "Me, too."

#

After the evening supper, Maggie, Matilda, Frankie's older sister Lydia, and cook Emily Johnson collected plates and serving dishes. Then they put leftover food into the larder* for the next day, scraped grease into the grease pot, and dumped the remaining scraps into a slop pail for the pig. Frankie and Chloe meanwhile filled two big tubs with hot water from the wash boiler* on the stove. Together they lugged each one to the table. While Frankie added soap to one of the tubs, Chloe went to the sink and got a swab* for the fine china and two washcloths for greasy dishes, pots, and pans.

Frankie enjoyed the evening routine. She liked how the different people in her household lived and worked peaceably together. She had come to love her unconventional family.

Her mother had a habit of bringing unlikely people into her boarding house. It was a habit that caused many of the town's people to shun Maggie. The first to arrive was Emily, who had been hired to do the cooking. After Emily and her carpenter husband Nate had been burned out of their home, Maggie invited the couple to live at the

Second Street Boarding House. Within a short time, Maggie and the woman with skin the color of café-au-lait became close friends, which scandalized those outside the family.

Nowadays the town gossips were busily whispering about the presence of four people of color living right on the town square and wondering just what Maggie Blaine Smith thought she was doing.

Frankie was proud of her mother despite all this because Maggie chose to do what was right rather than what was "proper."

Once the dishes had been organized on the table, everyone went to work. They washed the tumblers and teacups first, followed by the chinaware. Clean items were dipped in the rinse tub and set to drain on a rack. Next, they tackled the silverware, then the greasy dishes, and finally the pots and pans.

Frankie watched as her sister, mother, and friends chatted with one another. She thought about all the conversations she had that day. When there was a lull, she blurted, "Do you ever wonder why women don't get to do the same things as men?"

The other females blinked at her.

"Well?" she said impatiently. "Men go and fight. Men are allowed to have adventures. And men have exciting and dangerous work, but *we're* stuck in a house sewing and cleaning and cooking and caring for babies."

Maggie said, gently, "It isn't all that bad, Frankie. You'll see."

"But, Mama, it *is* that bad! What if I never get married? What if I want to have a career, like Papa? The only thing women are allowed to do is be wives or maids or cooks. The lucky ones get to be seamstresses, missionaries, or teachers. But what if I don't want to be any of those?"

13

Maggie took a breath. Her youngest daughter had never accepted the notion of "that's just the way things are." Although both of her daughters were intelligent and loved learning, Frankie seemed perpetually frustrated. Lydia had been able to move away way from being the family nurse to studying medicine with Dr. Lightner. Frankie, however, exploded with challenges that sounded off-putting and impertinent to those who didn't know her.

"You know," Frankie grumbled, "I think men just want all the good things for themselves."

"Frances," Maggie said, "Papa told me what happened between you and Patrick out on the porch."

Frankie looked appalled. "Papa's a gossip!"

"Do not call your stepfather names. He is *not* a gossip. He was concerned about you and it is clear to me that one of the reasons you're asking all these questions is because you don't want Pat to enlist in the army."

Chastised, Frankie stared at her feet.

Twenty-year old Lydia laid a sympathetic hand on her sister's arm. "I know how you feel. I'm upset about Edgar leaving. But Frankie, it is *his* decision. *My* decision is to stay here and continue learning with Dr. Lightner."

Frankie scowled. "What you're doing is important, Liddy! You'll be able to help wounded men when they come back home, and you'll be taking care of the ill and injured in our own town. But what can I do? I'm only sixteen."

Lydia smiled. "That's a perfectly normal question. When I was your age, I asked the same thing."

"But I want to be of help. Just like you." Frankie picked up a dinner plate and wiped it dry with a towel. "I wish girls could fight!"

Emily gasped. "Don't you ever wish that!"

"Why not?"

"Well, someone has to keep things running at home. Someone has to do the farming and the other

14

work. If many men join the army women will have to take over their duties. And who would raise the children if women enlisted?"

"But what if I'm not cut out for all that?" Frankie moaned, but quickly recovered and put the plate carefully in its place in a cupboard. "I keep feeling as if I'm called to do something else."

Maggie's heart skipped a beat. Both of her daughters had special gifts, and neither of their gifts was traditional women's work – especially the one she thought she saw in Frankie. That gift first emerged when her youngest daughter had stood up two years earlier at a camp meeting and "exhorted" the congregation. Now, everyone knew that exhorting was supposed to be comprised of words of encouragement, but Maggie and everyone else also knew that Frankie wasn't exhorting. She was preaching. She was interpreting the Bible and applying it to life, no matter how short her message had been. Women weren't supposed to do that. Women weren't supposed to be preachers.

But women were not supposed to be doctors, either and yet Lydia was learning medicine.

Confused, Maggie said a quick prayer that things would change enough for both girls to respond to their callings. Then she asked, "What do you believe you're called to do, my dear?"

"I don't know," Frankie shot back. "But I'm pretty sure it isn't this."

The other women gasped, all except Lydia who smiled lovingly at her sister. "Don't worry. God'll make it clear to you."

"Yeah? Well, I'd say God is taking his sweet time!"

"You watch your language, young lady," Emily scolded. "Don't you question the Almighty!"

Frankie sighed. "I'm sorry."

"You know, I believe God wants us to try things out." Maggie was eager to return to the subject at hand. "Frances, there are occupations you could try right here in Blaineton. I know you'd like to go to college and study theology, but until you're old enough for that, let's think about what else you can do. I heard today that our school is looking for someone to teach its youngest class. You helped with that group last year. Wouldn't you like to try being their teacher?"

"Maybe. I mean, I do like children."

"Well, then why don't we speak with the headmistress?"

Frankie nodded, but it wasn't a terribly enthusiastic nod.

#

That evening, Lydia stopped by the room that Frankie and Chloe shared. The two girls were dressed in their nightgowns. The windows were thrown wide open, allowing in a balmy evening breeze that carried with it the smell of greenery. Two small lamps shed a warm yellow glow over both the room and the young women. Frankie was engrossed in forcing her unruly red hair into a braid, while Chloe watched.

The sight of the two girls together reminded Lydia of the years she had spent sharing a room with her sister. The warm memories brought a smile to her lips. Together she and Frankie had shared secrets, fears, joys, and hopes. These things she now shared with her husband, Edgar – tall, blond, handsome, indigo-eyed Edgar, who, like Patrick, was about to enlist in the army.

At this, Lydia's heart made a little hitch and she involuntarily shivered. She did not want her husband to go and was afraid of what might happen to him. She also was afraid that her heart would shatter if something did.

She dreaded thinking about how she would live if he should die.

Lydia shook the feelings off and said to the two girls, "It's time to say good night."

When they smiled up at her, their innocence and promise touched her heart.

"Good night," Chloe chirped.

Frankie added, "'Night, Liddy."

Lydia sat down on the bed beside her sister. "Try not to worry about Patrick, please."

Frankie tied a strip of rag around the frayed end of her braid. "How can I not? And how can you not worry about Edgar?"

"Well, truthfully, I can't. I have no choice. I must worry. But I shall try to keep it at the back of my mind rather than at the front. Thankfully there are many other things to which I must attend. However, I will remember Edgar in prayer every day. Perhaps every moment," she added wistfully.

After a short silence, Chloe said, "Do you think we'll win the war, Liddy?"

Lydia took the young girl's dark hand in her pale one. "Don't be afraid, Chloe. If we lose, none of us here – and especially your mother - would ever let you go back to slavery. We would get you to safety in Canada if we had to carry you there on our backs."

The ten-year-old impulsively threw herself into Lydia's arms. "Oh, Liddy! I don't want to be a slave again!"

After kissing the braids on the child's head, Lydia whispered, "You will be safe. I promise." She then sat back and said to both girls, "Now, since you want to help with the war effort, I have a suggestion. Why don't you organize a group and roll bandages and scrape lint?"

Frankie cast her eyes heavenward. The very notion of sitting in a parlor, rolling up strips of cloth to be used as bandages and scraping, pulling, or raveling lint off old clothing to be used to pack wounds made her want to climb the walls. "That's all right for the likes of Mama, Emily, and Matilda. They're old. I want to *do* something!"

Lydia made an unsuccessful attempt to stifle a grin. "Well, then, you can always raise money to help our soldiers and the wounded. You and Chloe could arrange a fair."

"But that's so dull! There's a war on and here we are sitting at home."

"Someone has to stay at home, Frankie."

"Liddy, that is not an answer!"

Chloe chuckled. "I think Frankie wants to join the army!"

Straightening her shoulders, Frankie tried to look dignified. "Well, I *could* be a nurse! The army needs nurses, don't they?"

Lydia grinned. "Yes, it does, except Miss Dorothea Dix, Superintendent of Nurses will accept only women over the age of thirty-five and they cannot be attractive. *You*, Frances, just turned sixteen and are quite pretty."

Frankie frowned, got off the bed, and went to the mirror mounted over the bureau, where she gazed at her reflection. "Pretty?" She turned her head toward her sister and friend. "With *these* freckles?"

"Oh, you most certainly are pretty," Lydia corrected. "Your eyes sparkle, your nose is pert, and you have a pleasing figure."

"I'm short and skinny," Frankie countered. "And my figure is nothing like yours." She envied Lydia's ample bosom and round hips, not to mention her spotless skin, shiny chestnut hair, and wide dark eyes. Frankie gestured at Chloe. "And you! You have a beautiful smile and an adorable countenance! And you haven't even got your figure yet. No, I am perfect for Miss Dix's nursing corps!"

"You're still a child, my dear."

"Liddy!"

Lydia stood up. "I shan't argue any further with you." Dressing gown rustling, she went to her pouting sister and kissed her on the cheek. "You'll just have to figure out how you will help with the war effort on your own. Good night, dear sister."

Puckering her face, Frankie muttered, "Good night."

Lydia laughed and swept out of the room. Once she was down the hall and the door to her room had clicked shut, Chloe turned to her friend. "So, what *are* you going to do, Frankie?"

#

The day that Patrick and Edgar left to enlist at Camp Fair Oaks, Frankie was strong and composed, which surprised her beau greatly. She did not weep, pout, or storm. Instead, she smiled supportively across the table at him as they ate a farewell breakfast of eggs, potatoes, sausage, tomatoes, and biscuits. He wanted to ask what she was up to but decided not to risk it. He didn't think he could take a tantrum right before he was off to do the biggest, most dangerous, most important thing he'd ever done in his life.

As for Frankie, she was determined to keep a smile on her face. After all, she had a plan now and she was bound and determined to make it happen. Occasionally, when she glanced at her mother or her sister, she pitied them. They were stuck at home forever. Lydia was going to have to watch Edgar leave and then worry about him until the war ended or until he was mustered out.

Frankie also knew her mother would worry about her stepfather when he left. Granted, Eli Smith was not a candidate for the army. A wound received during the dark days of 1861 had left him with a limp and he got around now with the use of a cane. But despite his strong pacifist inclinations, he was editor of the *Gazette* and had decided that he and his assistant Chester Carson would follow the New Jersey Fifteenth Volunteers into the war.

Maggie had made it clear that she did not like Eli's decision. Unfortunately, her carefully worded opposition had done nothing to dissuade him. Soon she, too, would join the ranks of worried and praying women.

After their 5:45 a.m. breakfast, the men collected their carpet bags and the entire group of family and friends prepared to walk to the train station, where Eli, Maggie, Lydia, and Frankie would board the train with the two enlistees and accompany them to Flemington.

The plan was to catch the 6:20 a.m. Belvidere-Delaware Railroad train to Lambertville. Once there, they would disembark, board another train to Flemington, and arrive there at 10:30 a.m. Then the family would see the town, partake of a noon dinner at a restaurant, and finally walk the two young men to Camp Fair Oaks. After Patrick and Edgar enlisted, Maggie and her family planned to tour the camp and return to the depot in time to catch the 5:35 p.m. train home.

But right now, Frankie was standing on the front porch and watching Lydia and Edgar as they slowly strolled away from the house. She was proud of herself, for she felt strong and secure rather than worried and sad.

She turned when her mother and stepfather came out the front door.

"Frankie," Maggie said, "where is your bonnet?" Her mother was tying the ribbons of her own bonnet under her chin. "You'll need to wear it. The sun is strong today."

"I'll get it, Mama." Frankie ran back inside and plucked her bonnet from the peg by the door just as Patrick pounded down the stairs.

He stopped when he saw her and blushed. She was so pretty. He wanted to remember her like that. It was now or never, so Patrick blurted the speech he had been working on all morning. "Frankie, I just want to make sure you know that I care for you a whole lot. And I'm not trying to hurt you by joining the army."

She gave him the sweetest of smiles. "I know, Pat."

"And I'm gonna do my best not to get wounded. And I'll write to you as much as I can. I promise."

"Thank you. And I promise to write to you every day, too, even if it's only a few lines." She plopped her bonnet on her head and tied the ribbons under her chin in a sloppy bow. Then Frankie reached for his hand. "Come on."

Relieved, Patrick curled his hand around hers and marveled at the small feel of it. He suddenly felt protective of his girl and resolved to do his best to make sure the war ended in the North's favor. All he wanted was for her to be safe from harm.

"I hardly can believe it, Frankie," Patrick said as they walked onto the porch and down the steps. "You've had a change of heart."

"I just needed time to think things over, Pat."

When they got under the shade of the big tree on the square, Patrick leaned close and planted a kiss on her cheek. "You're being so brave, Frankie. I'm proud of you."

She smiled broadly, if not a bit mysteriously. "I'm proud of you, too." Standing on her toes, she kissed his cheek in return.

Up ahead of them, Maggie looked back at the house. She saw the two standing under the tree and smiled as she recalled the love she had for Frankie's father when they had been that young. It didn't bother her to see the two sharing a kiss. In fact, she waited a moment before calling, "Come along! We don't want to miss the train!"

Frankie had never been on a train before. It was fun to watch the world whizzing by the window at what surely must have been an unthinkable speed. She was seated next to Patrick and felt terribly grown up when he closed his hand around hers.

Across the aisle, she could see Lydia and Edgar sitting together. Her brother-in-law had his arm around her sister, and she was resting her head on his shoulder. Frankie observed them for a moment and then whispered to Patrick, "I do hope Liddy will have a baby."

"Why?"

"Because they've been married for over a year and a half and nothing's happened yet. I think a baby would be a good thing." A sad feeling came over her. "You know... just in case..."

Patrick nodded that he understood.

"It would be good to have a living part of Edgar around, wouldn't it?"

"Yeah." He looked her over with an expression that she found unsettling. "What about us?"

Frankie was appalled. "Pat! No!"

He laughed. "Not ready yet?"

"Not married yet," she primly replied. "And, besides, you're going to come back. I know it."

Her beau grew somber. "No one's guaranteed that, honey."

Honey? He had called her honey! Her stepfather called her mother "sweetheart" and Edgar called Lydia "dear." Now she had a pet name, too!

Frankie screwed up all the encouragement she could and said, "But you *will* come back. If I pray every day and you're careful, you'll come home."

22

Patrick chuckled again. "That's why I love you, Frances. You're so optimistic."

When they arrived in Flemington, everyone was trying to keep their spirits up with a fine dinner at a small restaurant. However, despite the good company and food, time was slipping away, and it was time to leave. As they approached Camp Fair Oaks, the family fell silent.

The goodbyes were awkward, painful, and melancholy. Lydia and Edgar clung to each other as long as they could, while Frankie and Patrick held hands and gazed into each other's face.

With a sigh, Maggie looped her arm through Eli's.

He gave her a smile. "They'll be fine."

"They're going to war," Maggie replied. "War is not fine."

"I won't argue with that. But both those young fellas want to come back. That's a powerful force."

"I pray God they will come back." Maggie turned sad eyes to her husband. The idea of him going away too was almost too much to bear. "And when do you plan to leave, Elijah?"

He shrugged. "Well, the *Gazette* has to obtain permission to go with the New Jersey Fifteenth. I'm confident we'll get it, but the government may not grant it for a month or so."

Maggie nodded. So, there it was. She had at least a month, a mere month, and then Eli would be gone, too. The house would feel strangely empty. So would her bed.

The white canvas of the camp's tents gleamed under the powerful August sun, beckoning the two young men to step into a new phase of their life. After a bit, they glanced at each other and nodded.

When the little party entered the tent for Company B recruitment, Edgar and Patrick gave their particulars to the officer and signed the corresponding papers. Once they had completed the process, the young man behind the desk smiled. "Thank you, privates. Report to the Quartermaster. He'll issue your uniforms and equipment to you."

"Yes, sir," the two said, attempting a salute.

The officer laughed and stood up. "Here's how you do it." He demonstrated for them.

The new recruits mimicked his motions and he nodded in approval.

The family walked out of the tent together and stood in the street in front of the line of recruitment tents.

Edgar cleared his throat and said quietly, "Well... I guess it's time." With that, he gathered Lydia up in his arms and they shared one last lingering kiss.

Patrick screwed up his courage and avoiding Eli's eyes, put his arms around Frankie and finally did what he had been longing to do – kiss her on the lips. All the while he could feel Eli's eyes boring into the back of his neck, but he didn't care. Frankie had met his lips without hesitation and, although it was the briefest of kisses, he knew he would treasure it until he returned.

"Elijah..." Maggie warned her glaring husband. "You are staring."

"But look at them," he whispered. "They're cavorting outside in front of God and everyone."

Maggie suppressed a smile. "A touch of the lips hardly qualifies as cavorting, my love."

"Well... it could *lead* to cavorting. I'm a man. I know."

Maggie cast her eyes upon her husband and murmured, "Do you, indeed?"

Patrick and Edgar picked up their bags, said goodbye to everyone, and then the two new soldiers walked briskly away, turned down the camp's main street, and disappeared.

"Mama," Lydia said softly, "if you don't mind, I'd rather not tour the camp. Not just yet."

"Of course, dear," Maggie replied. She took her daughter's hand. "Why don't we walk around town for a bit?"

As her family strolled away from Camp Fair Oaks, Frankie hesitated. She stayed behind to stare at the rows of white canvas and wonder what life would be like for Patrick and Edgar.

What *was* it like to be a soldier?

Well... there was only one way to find that out.

"Frankie," her mother's voice called. "Come along."

Shaken out of her reverie, she shouted over her shoulder, "Yes, Mama!"

After one last look at Camp Fair Oaks, Frankie spun around and ran after her family.

#

In the following days, everyone returned to their usual occupations. It was almost as if nothing had changed. Eli and Chester Carson continued to print the penny weekly newspaper with Maggie providing editorial assistance. Meanwhile, Matilda, Maggie, and Emily prepared meals and kept house. Emily's husband Nate was busy in his carpentry shop. Lydia walked to Dr. Lightner's house every day but Sunday and assisted him in caring for the town's people. And since it was summer and vacation from school, Chloe spent her time watching Maggie and Eli's adopted four-year-old son Bob and Nate and Emily's toddler son, Natey.

As for Frankie, having turned sixteen meant that she had completed her course of study at the little school in Blaineton. Free from books and essays, she now was given a greater share of duties: gathering eggs from the hens, milking the cow, cleaning the boarding house, helping prepare meals and doing the washing up that followed, and mending and doing laundry with the other women every Monday.

But even in the midst of that busy time, Frankie never forgot to write to Patrick and watch the mail for his letters. Patrick did not disappoint. The first missive from him arrived two days after he had enlisted and was full of descriptions of military life at Camp Fair Oaks. On their first day there, Patrick and Edgar had been issued uniforms, assigned to a tent where they lived with eight other men, and were drilled in marching and shooting, albeit with wood "weapons." In another letter, he told her that, among the military exercises, they had to bayonet straw dummies, which had made Frankie feel a bit queasy.

But Patrick mainly wrote about the men he had befriended, various officers and their quirks, the women who did laundry and those who cooked the meals and even included a line about women who provided other services. However, he was quick to note that he had no interest whatsoever in said services. Frankie wasn't quite sure what extra "services" women were providing but had heard about "painted women" and "hussies,"* so she figured it had to do with relations between men and women.

And then on August 18, a letter arrived with an extra bit of news: the regiment was nearly complete. Men from all over the surrounding counties had faithfully answered the call to serve the Union and almost all the ranks were full.

Frankie read the letter over several times by the light of her bedroom window. It was a stifling afternoon with scarcely a breath of air stirring. She could hear her mother talking to Matilda outside as the two women swept the front porch. Horse hooves clopped and wagon wheels clattered over the cobblestone street, providing background for their conversation. Frankie had heard these comforting sounds every day of her life, but now they seemed different as if they were calling her to something new. Everything around her was vibrating with change.

Frankie smiled, folded the letter, and hid it in the bodice of her dress.

#

Early the next morning, Frankie told her mother that she wasn't feeling well. Maggie cooed sympathetically and sent her daughter back to bed with a cup of tea.

After waiting until everyone else was busy in the kitchen, Frankie snuck up to the second floor of the old section of the house and slipped into Patrick's room. She closed the door just enough to prevent anyone from looking in and dropped a pair of well-worn gardening shoes, a pair of scissors, and a length of twine on the bed. Turning to the bureau, she stealthily slid a drawer open and rifled through Patrick's belongings. Eventually, she found a suitable pair of trousers and held them against her body. Smiling with satisfaction, she put them on top of the bureau and then pulled out a shirt and laid it on top of the trousers.

Next, she went to the wardrobe, where she retrieved a wide-brimmed hat made of brown wool felt. Patrick wore that hat when he went fishing or hunting. When she tossed it across the room, it landed neatly on the bed. Frankie grinned. She always had been good at skimming rocks across the river. She was glad she still had that skill.

Finally, Frankie picked up the scissors and turned to the bureau. After taking a deep breath, she steadied herself and grasped the braid into which her wavy, red hair had been woven. Then, biting her lower lip, she started cutting. Her hair was thick, requiring effort to get all the way through it, but within seconds the braid suddenly was in her hand and her head felt strangely light.

Frankie pursed her lips, set the braid on top of the bureau, and then turned the scissors to her head to even up the hair now hanging around her ears.

After a few minutes, she whispered, "Done!"

The image staring back at her in the mirror was that of a wide-eyed freckle-faced girl with bright hair waving about her ears and neck.

Satisfied, Frankie quickly shed her dressing gown and nightgown, revealing the chemise and drawers that she was wearing underneath. Then she reached for Patrick's trousers and stepped into them. She was grateful that she was slim, for they went easily up over her hips and buttoned neatly. Picking the twine off the bed, she wove it through the trousers' belt loops and tied it in the front to ensure that they wouldn't fall down.

Picking up Patrick's beige cotton shirt next, she shrugged it on, buttoned it up, and stuffed it into the trousers' waist. For once she was happy she didn't have much in the way of a bosom for, if she had been bigger, she would have been forced to bind her chest to keep it flat.

Finally, she grabbed the hat and plopped it on her head.

When she looked in the mirror this time the person staring back at her seemed more like a boy than a girl.

And then a small, shocked voice said, "Frankie, what are you doing?"

With a gasp, she whirled around.

Chloe, eyes wide, was standing in the doorway. "I thought you weren't feeling well."

"Close the door, please and keep your voice down."

Chloe shut the door behind her. "Why are you dressing like a boy?"

"Promise you won't tell?"

Chloe nodded.

"I'm joining up."

"Joining what?"

"The army, silly goose! Why else would I cut off my hair?" Frankie couldn't help feeling proud. "I'm going to Camp Fair Oaks today and I'm joining the army. I want to be near Patrick, and I want to do something for the Union. So, I'm going to fight with him side by side." She flopped down onto the bed. "But you can't say anything to anyone."

"What if they ask me? You know they will once they find out you're missing. I can't lie to them. Lying is wrong."

"Then say you don't know or shrug your shoulders." Frankie put on her old gardening shoes and stood up. "Well, how do I look?"

"Like a boy, I reckon."

"That's good because if they think I'm too young to be a soldier, I'm going to ask to be a drummer boy or a bugler."

Chloe looked skeptical. "But you don't know how to play either of those instruments."

Frankie thought a moment. "Well, I'm sure they'll teach me. People don't just show up knowing how to play the drums. I don't know anyone who plays the drums!"

"Mr. Pfeiffer does. He plays at parties and dances in town. And there's another man who plays the trumpet."

"Two men out of an entire town!" Frankie blew the information away with a wave of her hand.

"How're you gonna get to Flemington? You don't have any money."

"That's where you're wrong, Chloe! Remember how I helped with the little children at school?"

Chloe nodded.

"Well, the headmistress paid me for that, and I've got enough money to go to Flemington. When we took

Patrick and Edgar there, I heard the ticket master tell Papa how much it cost per person. So now I'm going catch the six twenty train."

"Well, you'd better hurry it's almost six o'clock now." Chloe frowned. "But, Frankie, maybe you should think things over."

"I already have thought it over, and I'm still doing it." She took a determined breath. "Look, I'm going out the front door. Could you go first and make sure no one's around? I think they should all be in the kitchen by now."

Chloe was uneasy at the notion of being an accomplice in Frankie's plan, but she sighed and said, "All right. Do what you must, but don't say I didn't warn you."

#

Shortly before noon, the women of the family were preparing dinner, the big meal of the day. Emily had made a hearty sausage stew, Matilda had cooked up greens with fatback, and Maggie had made biscuits. For dessert, Emily had whipped up fruit custard.

As she worked alongside the women, Chloe could feel her heart trying to pound its way out of her chest and was afraid everyone would be able to hear it. She knew, without a doubt that sooner or later Frankie's absence would be noticed. And what would she do then?

Unfortunately, they noticed Frankie's absence sooner.

After putting fresh, hot biscuits into a bowl, Maggie paused and said, "I think I'll check on Frankie."

"It's not like her to feel unwell," Emily commented. "She's usually healthy as a horse."

"I know. She didn't seem to have a fever." Maggie wiped her hands on her apron. "She did look a bit pale, though."

"You don't think her time of the month is coming on, do you?" Matilda asked.

Chloe wanted to drop through the floor. "Mommy!"

"Ain't no secret," Matilda said. "Everybody but you got one. And your time'll come."

Maggie smiled. "I don't think Frankie is unwell because of her monthly. But I do want to look in on her before everyone comes in for dinner."

Chloe's stomach twisted into a knot as she watched Maggie leave the kitchen. Hoping to appear as if everything was normal, she continued to lay silverware and plates on the table, all the while working to keep her hands from shaking and living in dread of what would transpire next.

Thirty seconds or so passed. Then Chloe heard the sound of Maggie's hurried footsteps approaching the kitchen from the hallway of the boarding house's new wing. Chloe squeezed her eyes shut and sent up a prayer for help just as Maggie burst into the kitchen.

"Frankie's not there!" Maggie was breathless and her eyes were wide. "Where could she have gone?"

"She's probably in the necessary,*" Emily said.

"I'll go look," Matilda offered and strode out the door to the back yard.

Emily was carefully ladling stew into a big serving bowl. Her café-au-lait skin glistened with perspiration. The day had started out warm, and the old wood-burning stove was making the kitchen close to unbearable. "Don't worry, Maggie. If she's feeling poorly she wouldn't be walking around town." Emily looked up suddenly. "Unless..."

"Unless what?" Maggie asked.

"Unless she fibbed about being sick."

"Oh, surely not, Emily."

"Now, Maggie, she *has* told little white lies now and then. It's only a small step to bigger things, you know."

31

Before Maggie could reply the back door flew open and Matilda blew in. "She ain't in the necessary. Where could that girl be?"

All of Maggie's maternal fears suddenly came to the surface and she was all but wringing her hands. "I don't know! Why would she tell me a lie?"

Shaking in her boots, Chloe stared nervously at the kitchen's gray-painted floor, hoping no one would say anything to her.

But someone did notice - her mother. Narrowing her eyes, Matilda crossed the room and stood in front of her daughter. "Why are you looking at your feet, girl?"

Chloe's lower lip began to tremble.

"Lift up your head."

Chloe did so and looked into her mother's face.

"You know something, don't you?

As tears stung her eyes, Chloe nodded.

"Then you tell us the truth right now."

"I can't, Mommy." Chloe began to sob. "I can't. I promised."

Maggie stepped in now. "Oh, my dear child, nothing terrible will happen if you tell us where Frankie is."

Chloe took up her apron and wiped her face.

"Please," Maggie said softly. "Tell us."

Chloe took a deep breath and finally brought her eyes up to meet Maggie's. "Frankie's run off, Mrs. Smith."

"Run off?" Matilda said with a frown. "Where to?"

"Flemington."

Emily raised an eyebrow. "Oh, so, she's gone to see Patrick, has she?"

"If she has, she is going to be very, very sorry," Maggie exclaimed.

But Chloe quickly said, "No. It's more than just going to visit Patrick, Mrs. Smith. She's run off to join the army so she can be with him all the time and fight for the Union."

A stunned silence hit the room.

The color in Maggie's face drained away as she tried to make sense of what the child before her had said. "She wants to join the army?"

Chloe nodded.

"But she's a girl," Emily sputtered. "She can't do that!"

"Frankie disguised herself as a boy. She cut off her hair and dressed in Patrick's clothes and his old fishing hat."

Matilda frowned. "Something got to be wrong with that child, I swear..."

Feeling a bit faint, Maggie sank onto a chair. After taking a breath to steady herself, she lifted her eyes to Chloe. "And you saw her before she left?"

"Yes, Mrs. Smith." Feeling terrible, Chloe now regretted that she hadn't reported Frankie's scheme the second she had learned of it. "She's run away."

#

"Now let me get this straight," Maggie's husband said as Chester Carson and Nate Johnson looked on. "Frankie ran away to join the army because she can't bear being separated from Patrick."

Wringing her hands, Maggie nodded. "And she wants to fight for the Union."

Carson calmly puffed on his pipe. "I find the younger generation these days to be terribly impulsive."

"Uh-huh," Nate agreed. "And they usually got no idea what they're doing."

Eli exhaled slowly. He sat for a second. Then he fished his watch out of his pocket and checked it. "It's noon. We've got just enough time to throw a few things in a bag and catch the 12:45 train." He glanced at his part-time reporter and typesetter. "You'd better come with me,

33

Carson. My guess is it'll take the both of us to get Frankie home."

"It'd be just like her to start hollering," Nate said. "That girl is liable to raise a ruckus on you."

Carson snorted. "Oh, marvelous. Then Eli and I will languish in jail for kidnapping. I scarce can wait."

Eli waved their talk off. "None of that is going to happen. What *will* happen is we'll bring her home where she belongs."

"There's no need for Mr. Carson to go with you, Eli," Maggie interjected as she began to remove her apron. "Frankie will behave if I go." She put the apron on the table and strode to the cast iron stove, where she stood on tip toe and retrieved a tin from the shelf above. Upon returning to the kitchen table, Maggie upended the tin and poured its contents onto the worn, oak boards of the tabletop.

Eli's eyes widened at the pile of coins. "Egad!"

"It's our pin money," Emily explained. "We save what we can for a rainy day."

Maggie, who had been counting, heaved a relieved sigh and pushed the coins back into the tin. "This is enough to get us to Flemington and back, plus a little extra for meals and a room in case we need them."

"You saved that much money?" Her husband lifted an eyebrow. "I think I'm gonna come to you the next time the *Gazette* needs a loan."

#

Flemington

Frankie had taken the train south, gotten off at Lambertville, and transferred to the train on the Flemington line. It was about 10:30 a.m. when she finally arrived in Flemington. She bounced onto the depot's platform and determinedly set out walking the mile or so to Camp Fair Oaks.

Her route took her through town and, since she had eaten nothing but a cup of tea very early in the day, Frankie was famished. She paused long enough to check the money in her purse and decided that she could get something to eat.

Finding a general store, she went inside and purchased a piece of cheese and a bun. Then she came back out into the growing heat of mid-morning, plopped down on the store's steps, and devoured her meal. When she was finished, she dusted off her hands, stood up, and walked on. She was quite pleased with herself and proud that she had taken things into her own hands.

Frankie's first view of the camp was the same sea of white canvas that she had seen when Patrick and Edgar had enlisted. A line of rectangular wall tents sat at the camp entrance. Behind them, conical-shaped Sibley tents were arranged in regular rows across what had been the county fairgrounds. Eli had told her that the enlisted men lived in the Sibleys and that the officers lived in wall tents.

Frankie contemplated the site for a few minutes. The encampment was enormous, almost like a town. Once she had joined the army, how would she ever find Patrick? No matter. She would. She was determined.

Looking around, Frankie spotted the tent into which Patrick and Edgar had gone to enlist. Squaring her shoulders, she marched over and entered its stuffy, dim interior.

Two blue-uniformed men were sitting behind a table. One of them motioned for her to come over.

Frankie did so.

"What're you doing here, son?"

Son! He thought she was a boy. So far, so good.

"I came to enlist," she said, deepening her voice as much as possible.

"Oh, you have, eh?"

"Yes. I want to be a soldier."

The men looked her over and snickered, which diminished her confidence.

"How old are you, boy?"

She defiantly lifted her chin. "Eighteen!"

The two erupted with laughter and nearly fell off their chairs.

The man who had spoken first recovered enough to say, "The hell you're eighteen. You're not over fourteen if you're a day."

"Fine. But that makes me old enough to be a bugler or a drummer, doesn't it?"

"It does, son, but I'm afraid you're too late. We're full up."

"Oh." Frankie's heart sank down to her feet. She hadn't anticipated this.

The second man said, "Look, you can walk around the camp all you want, but you gotta be outta here by sundown. Understand, boy?"

"Yes, sir. Thank you, sir." Sucking in her tears, Frankie hurried away before either man could notice that she was about to cry.

Her plan to enlist had collapsed. She did not have an alternative scheme. She was in a strange place. And, worst of all, she had burned her bridges so that she couldn't go home. Miserable, Frankie raced down the camp's main thoroughfare and, upon finding a patch of woods at the camp's edge, sought solace there. Curling up at the base of a tree, she began to sob.

After a bit, her courage returned, and she stopped weeping. Frankie reminded herself that crying was useless because it solved nothing. So, she sat under the shelter of the trees until an idea occurred to her: she needed to find Patrick or Edgar. They would know what to do.

Picking herself up, Frankie wandered back into the camp and stood at the junction of the main street and the smaller, perpendicular road at its edge. The main street was lined with tents to the left and right and was a hive of activity. Soldiers were everywhere, walking and chatting and laughing and lounging around the Sibleys. In the distance, she could hear the sharp crack of fire-arms and voices cheering and shouting.

Suddenly Frankie was alerted by chanting voices to her left. Turning her head, she saw a squad marching down the perpendicular street. And it was bearing down on her. Quickly hopping back to avoid the line of sol-diers, she nearly collided with an enormous tent, the sign in front of which said, "Mess."

She frowned. Mess? Had someone left a mess in-side? Why would anyone advertise a sloppy tent?

Curious, she peeked through the flap. As her eyes adjusted to the dim light, she saw lines of tables and benches. Obviously, people were supposed to sit at the tables. *That's probably where the soldiers eat,* she decid-ed, *but why call it a mess? Don't they clean up after they've eaten?*

Confused, she brought her head back out into the bright sunlight. Shading her eyes, she turned to her right and squinted down the perpendicular road. The march-ing soldiers were just making a sharp left turn and going down another street. Camp Fair Oaks ended several roads beyond it.

Outside the camp's boundaries a smaller encamp-ment was clearly set apart. In that area, Frankie saw cauldrons suspended over fires and groups of two to four women scrubbing and rinsing clothing, addressing stains, ironing, and mending.

Frankie's eyes widened. They were doing laundry!

Heartened to find other females doing a familiar task at Camp Fair Oaks, she wandered toward them. As she drew near, she saw a large sign that read, "Suds Row. No soldiers permitted!"

Although she was dressed as a boy, Frankie obviously was not a soldier and so figured it would be all right if she entered the women's encampment.

Once she entered Suds Row, she found more signs identifying which group of laundresses served which Company. Frankie quickly located Company B's tents. Three women were working there: a pale brunette, a suntanned blond, and a dark-haired girl with cocoa-colored skin.

Upon Frankie's approach, the brunette sharply lifted her head and squinted hazel eyes at her. "What d'you want, boy?"

"Nothing. I... I came here to enlist, but they told me I was too young."

The response made the blond laugh. She was buxom, round, and jolly. "Too young, eh? Well, boy, you better skedaddle. We ain't got time to hear your tale of woe. We gotta finish our work before sundown."

The dark-haired girl, skin glistening with sweat, said, "Oh, shoot, Lily, that ain't no boy."

"Says you," Lily replied.

"Yeah, says me. Ain't my problem you can't tell a boy from a girl."

"Well, now, *that'd* be a first for Lily," the brunette smirked.

As a blush crept its way from her neck to her face, Frankie protested, "I *am* a boy. Really!"

The dark girl chuckled. "No, you ain't. You're way too pretty to be a boy. And you got little titties. Skinny boys don't have titties."

Embarrassed, Frankie crossed her arms over her chest. She hadn't thought her bosoms were all that obvious.

"So, girlie, what're you doing dressed like a boy?" The brunette was squinting at her again.

"I don't know. I mean... what else am I to do? My beau enlisted and I wanted to come here to see him and... he's going to be leaving for the war... and... I don't know where he is... and girls aren't allowed to be soldiers... and..." A big tear suddenly slid down her cheek.

The brunette quickly got to her feet. "Oh, for goodness sake, don't cry." She came to Frankie's side and slipped an arm around her shoulder.

Frankie sniffed, pulled a handkerchief out of her pocket, and mopped her face.

"That's better. I'm Becky. What's your name?"

"Frances, but everyone calls me Frankie."

"Well, Frankie, welcome to Suds Row. We do the laundry for the regiment."

"And other things if they'd like," the blond added.

Becky glared at her. "Shut up, you. Ain't nobody's business what you get up to in your free time. Anyway, I got a suspicion Frankie here ain't no adventuress.* Probably pure as the driven snow from the look of her." She nodded at the blond. "That's Lily. She's all right if you ignore her tongue and her manner." She pointed at the dark girl. "And that's Rosa. She's colored."

"Just in case you hadn't noticed." Rosa rolled her eyes. "White people... I declare..."

"Hey! Watch your tongue!"

"Why don't you watch yours?" With that, Rosa scooped sudsy water out of a tub and splashed it at Becky, splattering it all over the chief laundress' apron. "Ha-ha! Got ya!"

But instead of getting angry, Becky laughed. "Why, you little so-and-so!" She scooped a handful of suds from Lily's tub and rubbed them onto Rosa's head.

Rosa shrieked, fell off her stool, and lay chortling on the ground.

Pushing her disheveled hair away from her face, Becky chuckled. "God protect me! I'm in charge of this lot and they're driving me crazy already!" She turned to Frankie. "So, you say your beau's in this regiment?"

Frankie nodded.

"Fine. Plenty of girls come here to visit their fellas. Couldn't you have done that without all the dramatics?"

Frankie sighed. "I wanted to join up and fight beside him."

That caused all three women to laugh loudly.

Lily said, "Once your monthly came on everyone'd know you was a girl. Takes a wily woman to hide that. We got one or two lady soldiers in this camp. But they're good at hiding it."

Rosa squinted curiously Frankie. "So, what're you gonna do now? You gonna go home?"

"No," Frankie replied, feeling miserable again. "I'll be in big trouble if I do."

"You really love your fella, huh?" Rosa said.

Frankie nodded.

"Look, I got an idea. What we're doing here is something for the war, isn't it? Laundry, I mean. These men ain't going nowhere without clean clothes. You could get a job with us, do something important, and see your beau all at the same time."

"Her?" Becky was skeptical.

"Sure. Why not? She's as good as anyone."

"Well, maybe it'd work." She turned to Frankie. "Lemme see your arms, girlie."

Frankie held out her arms.

Becky felt one and then the other and nodded. "You got muscle; I'll say that."

"Yeah," Rosa said. "I knew she could do this."

Becky considered the idea. "Well, we've only got three of us washing for Company B and we're allowed to hire four." She turned to Frankie again. "You can petition to join us if you want, but you'll have to pass muster and be fine with scrubbing your life away. You'll need to buy your own equipment, too. But you can share ours until you can afford to purchase what you need."

Frankie felt her heart begin to rise in hope.

Rosa sat back and, looking Frankie up and down said, "How old're you?"

"I turned sixteen in June."

"Yeah? I'm sixteen, too!"

The two girls exchanged happy grins, having discovered something in common in an uncertain environment.

Lily, however, wasn't at all sure about the idea. "I dunno, Becky. D'you really want to sign her up? We don't know nothing about her."

"Oh, why not? She wants to be near her beau and we sure could use another washer woman." Becky gave Frankie a nudge with her elbow. "I don't blame your wanting to be here, girlie. My husband joined four weeks ago, and Rosa's brother came in last week to work as a blacksmith. A lot of women in Suds Row got a man of one kind or another in the camp."

"Not me," Lily said proudly. "They let me in because I convinced 'em I was of good character."

Becky snorted.

Lily gave her a narrow-eyed glare. "Fine. Truth is I wanted to do something exciting. So far, though, that ain't exactly panned out."

"Don't worry, it'll get plenty exciting when we head south, so stop trying to make your own excitement." Becky turned to Frankie. "You know how to do the wash, don't you, girlie?"

"I sure do! My mama runs a boarding house."

"Would you like to be a laundress?"

Frankie took a breath. "If it'll keep me near Patrick and be something useful to our country, I'll wash my hands raw."

"Well, then, welcome to the Company B Laundresses! That is if the Quartermaster'll hire you. We'll ask him later. For now, why don't you help us so's I can see what you can do?"

Faster than she could count to three, Frankie found herself perched on a stool and bent over a 25-gallon oak tub full of water and suds. Becky shoved a soldier's shirt into her hands and, arms folded across her chest, stood over her.

Frankie smiled pleasantly up at Becky. Then she dipped the shirt into the water and vigorously scrubbed it over the wash board.

With a nod of her head and an approving grunt, Becky left Frankie and went to take the dry uniforms off a clothesline.

Rosa, who was working on removing grass stains from the knees of a soldier's trousers, paused to grin at the new laundress. "Well done!"

The redheaded girl laughed. "I've been helping my mother with the laundry ever since I was five years old. Mama says working is good for the soul." She dipped the shirt in the water. "I guess she's right. But I don't think it's all that good for either the back or the hands."

Rosa's grin widened. "Well, at least it pays."

Frankie's heart and mind suddenly swelled with the excitement and freedom that now lay before her. "Oh, Rosa! This is going to be such an adventure!"

The other girl's dark eyes saddened. "Yeah, but ain't you gonna miss your family?"

Frankie hesitated. "Well, of course, I will."

"If I was you and had a family and a home, I'd never leave. Ever."

"You mean you don't have anyone at all?"

Rosa shook her head. "No one except my brother, Jimmy. When he got hired on here as a blacksmith, I came along. I didn't have anywhere else to go. He's all I got, and I don't aim to lose him, not if I can help it." She returned her attention to the stain on the trousers. "You're lucky. I wish I had a whole family."

Without warning, a hollow little pit opened in Frankie's stomach. Her mother, her sister, her little brother, her stepfather, and all the other familiar faces in the boarding house soon would be no more than a memory. She worked to push the feeling away. "I know I'm lucky. But I can't sit at home and do nothing when this war is on. I don't aim to lose Patrick, either." And, bending forward, she began to scrub with renewed energy.

#

Later in the day, Becky sent Rosa and Frankie to deliver uniforms to two of their clients in Company B. As she trotted beside her new friend, Frankie noted that the street for Company B was almost at the other end of the camp. That was good to know. Now all she had to figure out was which Sibley tent was Patrick's.

She peered cautiously into the first couple of shelters but saw nothing and nobody each time. When Rosa stopped by the third tent on the left, Frankie sighed inwardly. *So much for snooping.*

"Laundry delivery for Privates Warner and McCarthy," the dark young woman called at the tent flap.

Two men, one with dirty blond hair and the other with stringy brown hair, came squinting into the sun light.

"Sergeant Warner?" Rosa asked.

The blond nodded. "Yep."

Rosa gave him his uniform.

Warner checked it over and nodded his approval. "Thanks."

"You're welcome."

"And you must be Sergeant McCarthy," Frankie said to the man with the stringy hair.

"Yeah, that's me." The man checked his clothing over, too, but made a face and said, "Still got a stain on one trouser knee."

43

"You rubbed it in real good," Rosa replied. "I worked on that stain for a good forty-five minutes. It's not coming out."

"You got a sharp tongue for a colored girl."

Warner chuckled. "She's got a sharp tongue for *any* girl."

"And proud of it," Rosa said.

"Yeah, and it's gonna get you in trouble someday."

McCarthy grunted and indicated Frankie. "So, who's he? And since when did we get a boy laundress?"

Frankie opened her mouth to say she was a girl, but Rosa spoke first, "Since this morning. His name is Frankie."

"Huh," McCarthy muttered, "why couldn't you get another girl like Lily?

Rosa said, "I think one Lily is enough for any Company, don't you?"

"Hell, no, she ain't enough. 'Side from Lily, all's you got is Becky. Might as well be talking to a Sunday school teacher."

"Becky's married."

"My meaning exactly. And I ain't interested at all in that skinny boy."

Rosa stared him down. "What about me?"

McCarthy laughed derisively. "I sure as hell ain't got no stomach for a tart-tongued little Negro like you!"

Eyes flashing, Rosa took a step toward the man. "Don't you dare call me a Negro!* I'm not a slave! I've *never* been a slave! I've always been free and you're a stupid whoremonger!"

"Why you little – " McCarthy seized her arm, causing the uniforms she was holding to fly everywhere. "Don't you ever speak to me like that!" He drew the other hand back to strike her.

Frankie dropped her pile of uniforms. Crying, "Leave her alone," she flew at him and grabbed his raised arm.

44

But McCarthy roughly threw her off and Frankie landed bottom-first on the ground with a teeth-jarring thud.

Fortunately, Warner intervened, saying in easy tones, "Aw, leave her alone, Fred. She's not worth it." He turned to the girls. "On your way now. Fred's got a bad temper. If you know what's good for you, you won't give him no more sass."

Frankie picked herself off the ground. Both girls straightened their shoulders, gathered the clean uniforms from the ground, and marched away, feet churning up the dust on the dirt street.

Lips tight, Rosa put a hand on the spot where McCarthy had grabbed her and rubbed her arm.

"Are you all right?" Frankie asked.

Rosa nodded, but her eyes glistened with tears.

"Let's go back to Suds Row." Frankie put an arm around her new friend's shoulders.

Rosa took a big breath. "No. We gotta make our deliveries. It's our job." After a moment, she cast a sidelong glance at Frankie. "Know what? From now on when I deliver Private McCarthy's uniforms, I won't say boo to him. Instead, I'm just gonna imagine I'm sticking a bayonet in his big ol' gut." She snorted. "Men like him think every woman ought to be like Lily."

"Are there many laundresses like her?"

"No! And, anyway Lily ain't all bad. She just likes to have her fun. What she's really trying to do is find herself a husband."

Frankie considered this. "Yeah, but I can think of better ways to do *that*. As my Mama says, why buy the cow when you can get the milk for free?"

When Rosa laughed, Frankie smiled. She had helped her new friend feel better.

#

Lambertville

Maggie and Eli had rushed to catch the 12:45 train from Blaineton, only to find that the journey would take longer than anticipated. After they reached Lambertville depot, they learned that the train to Flemington would not leave until 5:35 p.m.

There was nothing else to do for the next hours save worry, so Eli sought to ease Maggie's anxiety by taking her on a walking tour of Lambertville, which compared to Blaineton was a bustling city.

Maggie, however, was not the least bit interested in learning about the river town.

Despite her lukewarm response, Eli gamely escorted her to the Delaware River. As they walked along the shoreline, he pointed southward. "All along here are factories. The first building houses the rope and twine factory. Past the Swan Creek, there's a car house, repair shop, and paint shop belonging to the railroad."

"Mm," she replied.

"And off to the north," he turned and pointed in the opposite direction, "there's a grist mill!"

Maggie nodded.

Undeterred, Eli took her arm. "Let's walk up Bridge Street, shall we?"

"If you wish."

They climbed up the embankment and found their way back onto Bridge Street. As they strolled along, Eli pointed out the other factories and then told her all about the factory north on Elm Street that made wheel spokes. Hoping to give her a perspective, he said, "They roll out more wheels than your brother's factory. Good thing there's more than enough work to go around, thanks to the war. That is if it's possible to thank a war."

As they continued up the street, Eli told her about the bank and then paused in front of a hotel. "Ahh, there she is! Lambert's Inn. Built in 1812. Would you like to take supper there?"

Maggie shrugged.

Having done everything to get her involved in the glories of Lambertville, Eli now was forced to resort to cajoling. "Oh, come now. Cheer up, sweetheart. Frankie is far from helpless. She'll have an adventure, we'll find her, bring her home, and subject her to a suitable punishment."

A droll smile touched the corners of Maggie's mouth. A "suitable punishment..." It was almost impossible for her to stay annoyed at her husband when he used wording like that. "My dear husband, I believe what you're actually saying is that there is nothing for it but for us to take a meal."

"That is precisely what I'm saying, particularly since we skipped dinner!"

Maggie chuckled. "Then I suppose we must dine. I can't have you fainting on the train to Flemington, can I, my love?"

"No, you certainly cannot, Mrs. Smith." And he led her up the steps to the Inn.

#

Flemington

"Let's go," Becky ordered.

Sweaty and with hands already red from exposure to water, soap, and scrubbing, Frankie got up from her stool and stretched her back. "Where are we going?"

"To see the Quartermaster."

Becky set off at such a fast pace Frankie had to trot to keep up with her. "Do you think he'll hire me?"

"Can't say. But they promised us one more woman and, well..." She gave the young redhead an appraising glance. "You're almost one."

"Thank you," Frankie replied, although she wasn't sure whether the comment was approving or dismissive.

The Quartermaster's tent was outfitted with a desk and chair, a cot, a table with two more chairs, a bookcase, and a trunk. The Quartermaster himself was short with a ruddy complexion, white hair, and a bushy white beard. And he was nearly invisible behind the stack of ledgers on his desk.

"Sir?" Becky said.

The man looked up and frowned. "Yes?"

"I'm Rebekah Mills, chief laundress for Company B."

"Yes?"

"We currently have three women for the whole company and this young lady turned up today and –"

"Young lady?" he interrupted. *That's* a young lady?"

"Yes, sir. She thought she would join up to be with her beau, sir."

The Quartermaster sniffed. "She must be the third one this week. I think we've caught them all, though."

"Yes, sir. I hope so, sir. My point is this is Miss Frances Blaine. I tried her out at our station, and she knows laundry, sir, and she's a hard worker. Would it be possible to hire her as our fourth laundress?"

A long, weary sigh hissed from between the Quartermaster's teeth. "Are you having trouble getting your work done Miss Mills?"

"Mrs. Mills, sir. My husband is a private in Company B. And, yes, sir, we are having some difficulty, as the company is filling up."

The Quartermaster's watery blue eyes swept over Frankie once again. "This one sure looks like a boy." He glanced at Becky. "Well... do you believe that this... *young lady* is of good character?"

"Yes, sir, and I'll make sure she stays that way."

The Quartermaster shoved a piece of paper and a pen across his desk and toward Becky. "Write a statement attesting to that effect and sign it."

With a nod, Becky bent over the desk and did as he requested. Then she stepped back to stand by Frankie's side.

After reading the statement over, the Quartermaster sighed once more. "Fine." He brought his head up and met Frankie's eyes. "Come here, missy."

With a shove from Becky, Frankie stumbled over to the desk. The Quartermaster opened yet another ledger and laid it before her. "You will receive seventy-five cents per month per each enlisted man's uniforms." With a glance at Becky, he added, "I take it she will not be doing officer's uniforms?"

"That is correct, sir," Becky replied and then said to Frankie, "You could earn as much as seven dollars and fifty cents a month if you work hard and can find ten enlisted men who can afford your services."

Seven dollars and fifty cents a month seemed like a tremendous amount of money. Frankie tried not to grin.

"Are you able to write?" the Quartermaster was asking her.

"Of course," Frankie replied, and remembered to add, "sir."

"Excellent. Write your name on this line." The man jabbed a finger at a spot on the page labeled, "Company B Laundresses." He dipped a pen in the ink well and handed it to her.

"Thank you, sir." Frankie took the pen and scratched her name in sloppy cursive on the line.

"Very well, Miss... eh..." He glanced at her name. "Miss Blaine. Welcome to the Army."

Beaming, Frankie thanked him and would have said more, had Betsy not seized her arm and hauled her out the tent's flap.

#

The train arrived at the Flemington depot with a jolt and a squeal of brakes. When the cars finally came to a halt, a weary-looking Maggie alighted onto the platform, followed by Eli, who was carrying a carpet bag. After glancing around, they located the station master, a man with a long nose and scraggly beard.

"Pardon me," Eli said, "we've come to visit a family member who's at Camp Fair Oaks."

"Oh," the Station Master replied, "I'm afraid you'll have to do that tomorrow morning, sir. The camp closes to the public at six o'clock."

Maggie was crestfallen. "I see."

"But it opens to the public promptly at eight o'clock tomorrow morning."

"Well, then," Eli said, "perhaps you could point us to a guest house where we could lodge for a night or two."

"It so happens that my sister has one. She runs a clean house and provides fine food. And she has a spare room tonight."

Maggie's spirits immediately were buoyed. "Thank you."

"Her house is on Bonnell Street. It's called Pleasant Rest, which indeed it is."

After thanking the man, Eli and Maggie stepped into the streets. The town's lamplighter had completed his job early. The lamps' small yellow flames were burning already.

"I hope Frankie is safe tonight," Maggie said as they walked.

Eli gave her a reassuring smile. "She'll be fine, sweetheart. You've raised a resourceful young woman."

"I daresay a bit too resourceful."

"And we'll just have to trust in that resourcefulness. Don't worry. We'll find her tomorrow."

#

That night the laundresses took supper in the mess tent, although they sat apart from the soldiers. Becky promised to get Frankie her own plate, bowl, cup, and cutlery in the morning and suggested that she share Rosa's mess kit. To Frankie's great relief, Rosa cheerfully obliged.

Supper consisted of lamb stew and biscuits. There was strong coffee to drink and ripe, juicy peaches to eat afterward. Throughout the meal, Frankie kept craning her head, hoping to see either Patrick or Edgar. To her great disappointment, though, she could find neither amid the sea of blue uniforms.

Disheartened, she trudged back to Suds Row with her fellow washerwomen and helped them clean up the day's work and fold dry uniforms. Then they ironed the officers' uniforms and laid them out on a table in Becky's tent to be delivered early the next morning.

Once the sun went down, they sat around the fire and chatted. Suddenly a soldier approached. Not very tall and on the thin side, he was carrying a uniform wrapped in a ball under one arm. Since soldiers weren't permitted in Suds Row, he had traveled surreptitiously behind the tents and now waited in the shadows.

After a few minutes, Becky acknowledged the person. "Well, hey, there, Bill." She stood up and joined him in the darkness by the tent. "Nice to see you."

"Nice to see you, too, Becky." The soldier's voice was a husky tenor.

Intrigued, Frankie watched as the soldier passed the bundle to Becky. She couldn't help but notice the small size of the soldier's hands and was amazed at the way he had flouted breaking the rules by personally delivering his clothes to Suds Row. Normally, enlisted men were ordered to set their dirty laundry outside their tents.

"Got some special items inside my bundle," Bill said.

Becky nodded. "They'll be clean and ready to use again in four days. We'll tuck them inside the uniform as usual."

As the two continued to chat, Frankie whispered to Rosa, "What special items?"

"Women's rags." She tugged on the sleeve of Frankie's shirt. "Come on."

Once the two girls were standing by Rosa's tent, Frankie whispered, "So what did you mean by women's rags?"

"I mean that soldier's no man."

Frankie's mouth fell open. "He's a woman?"

Rosa nodded. "We clean the monthly rags she uses and give 'em back wrapped in a uniform. No one's the wiser.""

"A real woman soldier..." Frankie stared at Bill in awe.

"Yep. Looks the part, doesn't she?"

"Does she have a beau or a brother here?"

"None that I know of."

Frankie frowned. "Why would she bother enlisting then?"

Rosa shrugged. "I don't know. Maybe she wants money. Or maybe she wants adventure or feels patriotic or something. Bill lived on a farm and has three brothers and seven sisters. She probably just wanted to get out of there. Claims she can work a farm and shoot better than any man and most soldiers. And she's good with a bayonet. I saw her practicing once."

Frankie's head was spinning. The information was new and a bit uncomfortable. Yet, as she watched the soldier talk and laugh with Becky, she also experienced a twinge of envy. "I wish I had her freedom."

"How come?"

"Everyone keeps telling me what I ought to do and what I can and can't do. But no one ever explains why. All they do is say it's because I'm a girl or I'm sixteen or it just isn't done. Those things aren't answers as far as I'm concerned. I mean, why can't I join the army? Why can't my sister be a doctor? Why do only a few colleges accept girls? What's the matter with women that we aren't allowed to do things like that?" She frowned. "Do you think it's because we get monthlies and have babies?"

Rosa shook her head. "Why does my being colored keep me out of most jobs? Why does it cause me to get paid less than white women? White folks say we're stupid and shiftless, but they don't know us. And you know what's worse? They don't even *try*."

Frankie put an arm around Rosa's waist. "Well, *I* know a couple things about you. You work hard and you're clever. And I'll take on anyone who says otherwise."

Rosa smirked. "Like you tried today?"

"Yes. Only I hope I do a better job if there *is* a next time."

Rosa gazed into her friend's eyes for a moment. "You're not the usual white person. I like that."

"My Mama says we're all the same inside. Anyway, we're the same age. We need to stick together."

"And we need to be honest with each other no matter what."

"No matter what," Frankie agreed.

The two shook hands on the deal. When Frankie returned her gaze to the soldier, she noticed that Bill was looking in her direction. She abruptly remembered that she still was wearing boys' clothing and, yet, the expression on Bill's face told her that she recognized Frankie for what she was and that the two of them shared a secret.

Once Bill slipped back into the shadows, the laundresses retired for the night. Rosa offered to share her tent with Frankie.

Rosa had made the tent a little home of her own with two cots, a small trunk, and a clothesline. The cot was neatly made up with clean, white sheets and a pillow in a crisp white case.

Frankie watched as her new friend cast off her waist, skirt, and petticoat and put on a nightgown. She shed her underthings beneath the cover of her gown and then hung everything up to air overnight on the line strung across the tent.

Suddenly Frankie felt ill-clothed and ill-prepared to be a laundress. Her boy's clothing was already dirty. The cot she was supposed to sleep on had only a sheet-less, stained mattress. She wondered how long it would take to earn enough money to purchase girls' clothing, a pillow, and sheets, not to mention the items she needed to be a full-fledged laundress.

As if she could read Frankie's mind, Rosa said, "We can buy you new clothes once you get your first pay." She smiled. "And, you know what? It's summer. The evenings are warm. I don't need my top sheet. Why don't you take it until you get things of your own? I've got an extra nightgown you can borrow, too."

After receiving the items from Rosa, Frankie removed her outer clothing and pulled the nightgown over her head just as Rosa had done. She removed her chemise and drawers under the gown's modesty-shield, popped her arms through the nightgown's sleeves, and then draped her own clothing over the line, put the sheet on her mattress, and got onto the cot.

Rosa put out the lamp. "Good night."

"Good night." Frankie realized how bone-weary and emotionally exhausted she was.

Once she was alone in the dark with her thoughts, though, she was besieged by melancholy. She had never been away from her family – not ever. Now she was working as a laundress and disguised as a boy. Patrick was somewhere in the camp, but where? Soon they would all be marching far, far away and she wouldn't see her mother, stepfather, sister, or little brother, or any of the other people who lived in the boarding house for a long time. Maybe never. She was truly on her own. Very soon the people she loved would be a memory.

Stop it, she thought. *This is what you wanted, isn't it?*

Of course, it was.

But another part of her mind whispered: *Then why is it everything doesn't feel exciting and new anymore? Why is it strange and empty and unsettling?*

She remembered the time she had spoken up at camp meeting. She would miss camp meeting in September. Maybe she'd never be able to speak at a camp meeting again. She'd miss that, even if people did stare at her as if she had two heads. And then she thought of the theology books the Rev. Mr. Madison had bequeathed to her. She'd never be able to read them again.

But, anyway, the books and the speaking didn't really matter, did they? It wasn't as if she could be a minister. Women were not allowed to be ministers. Just like she was told women couldn't be soldiers.

Frankie frowned in the dark. Why was it she was always told she "couldn't" do the things she was interested in?

Abruptly, without warning, she missed her mother. And she missed Lydia, and Emily, and Chloe, and her stepfather... She would miss being told that she "couldn't" because they never said it to be mean. They were trying to teach her, even if she didn't appreciate what they were trying to do. And now she wouldn't hear those voices again for a long, long time. And what if one of them should die before she returned home? How terrible that would be!

Tears stung Frankie's eyes and she tried to stifle a sob with her hand.

A soft, confident whisper to her left said, "Don't cry, Frankie. Everything's gonna be all right."

"Oh, Rosa," she whispered, "I miss my Mama!"

"You can always go home. It's not too late."

"I can't." Frankie was all torn up. "She must be so disappointed with me. I can't face her. I know she loves me no matter what, but I would be embarrassed." She turned on her side to face her new friend. "Did you feel this way at first?"

"Not when I came *here*. But I hurt real bad when my mam died. It was terrible, worse than when Pap died. The only one left was my brother." Rosa took a deep breath. "We're supposed to stay with our family until we're old enough to live on our own. Some of us try to leave earlier and sometimes we end up going back home. Other times something terrible happens so we can't go home. And sometimes we do just fine. But there are times when things happen – when we have to leave our families or get left alone because folk die. That's what happened to me and my brother. Frankie, if I had my druthers, my mam and pap'd still be alive, and we'd all be together." She sighed. "I guess you can't always have your druthers, can you?"

Frankie sniffed. "I suppose not."

"Listen, you might do just fine all on your own. That's for you to decide. But in the meantime, you're here with me." Rosa reached a hand out to her.

Smiling through her tears, Frankie did the same and took Rosa's hand in hers.

"It's important to have friends, no matter what you decide. And we're friends, right?"

"Right."

56

"Good," Rosa said. "Now, we'd better go to sleep. Dawn comes mighty early, and we've got another long day ahead of us."

#

Mrs. Clamp, the proprietress of the Pleasant Rest Guest House, escorted Eli and Maggie to their room. On the way, she was every bit as cheerfully chatty as she had been over tea. "I was in Blaineton once. Such a lovely little town!"

"Thank you," Maggie replied. "Do you have family there?"

"A cousin and her husband. They had just welcomed their first child and I traveled there to help care for the infant." She turned and smiled. "It was a boy. A fine, fat boy!"

Maggie smiled. "I am glad to hear it was a healthy child."

"Oh, yes." She chuckled. "Of course, he has been joined by two sisters and a brother since. What brings you to Flemington, Mrs. Smith? Do you have family here?"

"Not as such. We're visiting someone at the camp. He was part of our boarding house and we want to wish him well before the Regiment leaves."

His scrupulously honest wife seldom fibbed. Glancing at Maggie, Eli raised one eyebrow in surprise.

She met his gaze with an expression that he clearly understood to mean, "We shall talk about this later."

Clearing his throat, Eli stepped away from his wife and into the bedroom. "Why, Mrs. Clamp! This chamber is exceedingly comfortable."

As the proprietress lit a lamp on the bureau for them, Maggie said, "Patrick is almost a son to us. Why he's been at my boarding house since he was a lad of fourteen and just starting an apprenticeship."

"I am surprised an apprentice could pay for lodging at all," Mrs. Clamp commented.

"Ah, well, he couldn't under normal circumstances, I'm sure," Maggie said. "But when I learned that his employer had him sleeping in a drafty outbuilding, I took him in for a price he could afford."

Mrs. Clamp smiled warmly at her. "I daresay that wasn't very much."

"Oh, it wasn't," Eli added. He threw a grin in Maggie's direction. "But as my wife constantly reminds me, money isn't the only valuable thing in this world."

"So true, Mr. Smith, so very true. I have done much the same for some of my visitors." Mrs. Clamp lifted her lamp and said, "Well! Breakfast is at 7:00 in the morning. Would you like me to rap on your door to 'rouse you?"

Maggie shook her head. "No, thank you. We will rise with the sun."

"Then I shall see you in the dining room at 7:00. Sleep well." And Mrs. Clamp shut the door behind her.

Although they finally were without an audience, it wasn't until Eli and Maggie were in their bed clothes that they began to speak. "Would you like me to brush and braid your hair, sweetheart?" he asked.

Maggie nodded and, with a smile, sat on the edge of the bed and let her hair down.

Her husband got behind her and began to work a brush through her long, auburn hair.

She laughed lightly. "You do so love this."

"It's because it gives us a chance to talk." He leaned over and whispered in her ear. "And you've got such beautiful hair."

Maggie rewarded him with a kiss. "You're wonderful. I'm lucky to have you as a husband."

Eli returned to brushing. After a minute or two, he said, "Maggie?"

"Mm?"

"Why did you fib to Mrs. Clamp?"

"Why did you fib to the station master?"

Eli laughed. "I didn't fib, Mrs. Smith. I merely withheld information. I told him we were looking for a family member, which happens to be true. But you, Mrs. Smith– "

"I," Maggie interrupted, "knew Mrs. Clamp would want more. Women crave details."

"Margaret! I'm a man and *I* crave details."

Maggie turned her head toward him. "*You* are a newspaperman, Mr. Smith."

"Indeed I am. But curiosity is not the sole purview of women."

"Fine. Then I shall confess. It was embarrassing to admit to strangers that my daughter has run away."

"Why?"

"I feel a failure. What did I do to cause her to run off?"

Eli tenderly kissed her neck. "You did nothing, Margaret, and you are *not* a failure. Frankie is a handful. Always has been."

"Perhaps I've been too lenient."

He chuckled. "You've been perfect. Not too hard, not too soft." He began to weave her hair into a braid. "You're afraid for your little girl, Margaret, but you needn't be. Frankie is going to be just fine."

Maggie was silent.

"We'll find her tomorrow. I promise."

"I pray that will be so."

Leaning forward, Eli kissed her on the cheek. "Then pray. You're good at praying."

"Only if you pray with me."

"I will, but I'll pray in silence. I cannot do otherwise. My mother raised me to be a good Quaker, and although I'm no longer affiliated with a Meeting, that one thing remains."

She smiled. "I think more than one Quakerly thing remains, Eli. Your distaste for violence and war, for example."

He grinned. "Egad, you've found me out. Let me finish your hair, sweetheart. Then we'll pray together."

#

The next morning, Frankie went to breakfast by herself. The laundresses had a great deal of work to do and so decided to eat their meals in shifts.

Once in the mess hall, Frankie found an empty table that was a distance from the soldiers. After sitting down, she said a quick prayer to thank God for her food and took a sip of coffee. The brew was good and strong. She liked coffee. It was a rarity now the war was on, and she was glad most of the coffee was going to the soldiers, for they deserved even a small kindness like a stimulating drink in the morning. And, in all truthfulness, she was glad to have coffee that morning, too, for she had not slept at all well.

Her dreams had been unsettling and anxiety-provoking. Even though she couldn't remember them, they had awakened her while it was still dark, leaving her disturbed and moody.

Frankie had tried praying, but it was no good. Her mind wouldn't settle on God – especially when she realized that she had left her Bible back in Blaineton. Now she had one more thing to purchase with her yet-to-be-received pay. She wondered if perhaps a Bible should not be the *first* thing to purchase. In its pages, she found inspiration and hope, so it certainly would be of more immediate value than a dress or sheets.

Suddenly someone sat down beside her, and Frankie emerged from her reverie with a little gasp. Once she focused on her companion, she found it was Bill, the female soldier she had seen the other evening.

"Morning."

"Good morning," Frankie stammered.

"My name's Bill. Private Bill Crenshaw."

"You aren't supposed to be speaking with someone from Suds Row," she said.

Bill took in Frankie's hair and clothes and smiled faintly. "If I'm not wrong, I think that applies only to girls. How comes a boy like you's working with the laundresses?"

Frankie blushed and whispered, "Because I'm not a boy."

Bill nodded.

"But you knew that about me last night. How'd you know?"

"One woman knows another around here. So how comes you're dressing like a boy?"

Frankie dug into the scrambled eggs on her plate and shoveled a forkful into her mouth. Eating gave her a chance to think. "Well, my beau is in Company B and I was going to enlist so I could be with him, and so I could do something for the Union. But the recruiters said I looked too young. When I said I could be a bugler or a drummer, they told me they already had enough. Now I'm working with the laundresses. I've got to stay a boy until I can buy other clothes, and that won't be until I start drawing my pay."

Bill nodded and took a bite of biscuit. "Actually, I *like* being dressed like this. No petticoats and skirts. Nothing to trip you up. Don't you like that feeling?"

"I do," Frankie agreed. "And I despise crinolines and corsets."

"So why do you want to go back to dressing like a girl?"

She shrugged. "Habit, I guess."

"Well, it's more than clothes for me. I mean," Bill leaned close, "I can do whatever I choose when I dress like this, just so long as I can actually do it. That's the only limit for men. Can you imagine the freedom of that?" She sat back, looking thoughtful. "You know, I just might keep on being a man after the war's over."

Frankie considered Bill's comments. It had never occurred to her that a girl might masquerade permanently as a boy. Her mother probably would say it was deceptive to be something or someone you weren't. But who was it hurting if Bill posed as a man? If it didn't hurt anyone, how could it be wrong? She glanced at the soldier. "What will you do after the war?"

Bill shrugged. "I dunno. Work in a mill, maybe. Or head out west." She chuckled. "Hell, I could even go back to farming!"

"You know, you can probably dress as a man and be anywhere. Why'd you decide to join the army?"

Bill gazed into the distance. "There was nothing for me at my father's farm. And we needed the money – I got seven sisters and three brothers plus our ma. My pa got into debt buying some cows, see. He's always been terrible with money. So, one day, when I went to town I saw the flyer saying they was looking for soldiers. They paid real good money to sign up and good pay after. Now I'm able to help my family and make some money of my own. Maybe I'll even make a name for myself. Well, a name for Bill Crenshaw at any rate."

Bill had a strong, tanned face, short dark hair, and narrow, steel-gray eyes. In a uniform, she looked like a young man in his teens. For all anyone could tell, Bill was just a beardless teenage boy.

"How old are you?" Frankie asked.

"Seventeen. You?"

"Sixteen." After a little pause, Frankie blurted, "How do you hide it?"

"Hide what?"

"You know. Being... well... being a woman."

Bill laughed. "Aw, hell, it's easy. I'm wearing trousers. 'Long as you got trousers on, men think you're one of them. I don't bathe with them or use their necessaries, but they just think I'm being modest 'cause plenty of the other men bathe and care for themselves in private. One of the men in my tent did laugh at my feet, though. Said they was too small for a boy. Was he ever surprised when I knocked him into a cocked hat!" She grinned naughtily and for a second Frankie could see the teenage girl beneath the disguise. "They had to pour water on him to bring him round. He was bigger than me, but hell it was easy! See, I used to best my brothers all the time. That fella was easy pickings." Bill took a swig from a tin coffee cup. "Don't you tell nobody about me, understand? Only the laundresses know."

"Oh, I won't tell anyone," Frankie promised. She stared at her plate of potatoes, eggs, biscuit, and scrapple* for a moment. "So, no one else really knows?"

"Nah, they don't suspect a thing. I can do everything a man can do and I'm wearing trousers, so they don't bother looking too close."

When Frankie brought her eyes up, she found that Bill was studying her. She frowned. "Why're you looking at me?"

"'Cause I'm thinking you're better off with the laundresses." Bill teasingly nudged her with an elbow. "Somehow I just can't see you hauling a musket around. No, sir. Not at all."

#

When Frankie returned to Suds Row, Becky immediately sent her to deliver an armload of clean uniforms. The chore lifted her spirits. As she walked around the camp, she reveled in the sweet morning air. At last, she had a chance to find Patrick.

She made her final delivery to a pimply young man. After he had received his uniforms, she said casually and in her best tenor voice, "Say, do you happen to know which Sibley is Private Patrick McCoy's? He's a friend of mine from home."

"Sure!" The young fellow pointed across the street. "That one there. That's his."

"Thank you kindly."

Elated, Frankie wanted to fly across the street but forced herself to walk. After all, she didn't want to look too eager.

It took her aback when she called out to Patrick through the tent flap only to be told by a brusque voice within that he wasn't there, that the rest of them were sleeping, and that she needed to leave them the hell alone.

"Um..." she stammered. "Thank you?"

"Just do us a favor and shut your pan*," another voice growled.

"Yeah, go saw your timber*," another snarled.

Frankie blew out a long breath as she thought, *Well, that isn't very nice. What ever happened to manners?*

Turning, she looked around at her surroundings. *Now, what?*

And that was when she heard a noise. It was the familiar slop-slop-sloop of water in a tub and it was coming from behind the Sibley.

Curious, Frankie wandered toward the sloshing and discovered Patrick, shirtless, hunched over a wash tub and board, and scrubbing one of his uniforms.

"Pat?"

64

He looked up and frowned.

She pulled her hat off. "It's me."

His mouth dropped open. "Frankie?" He staggered to his feet. "What're you –"

Before he could finish the sentence, Frankie ran at him and threw her arms around his neck.

"Where's your hair?" he stammered.

"I cut it off."

"I can see that much. Why?"

Frankie let go and stepped back. "I was planning on joining up."

"Joining up? You?"

"Yes! But they told me I was too young."

"And too female! Frankie, what were you thinking?"

Embarrassed and disappointed at his response, she said, "I want to do something for the Union. And I want to be with you."

"Well, you can't. It's too dangerous."

"It's dangerous for you, too! And what if something happens to you? I want to be there to help."

With a sigh, Patrick put his arms back around her. "Oh, Frankie, you're crazy as a bedbug, but I love you. I really do."

A movement off to the side suddenly caught Patrick's eye. Squinting, he found one of his tent mates, Private Paul Schmidt watching them. Abruptly he held Frankie out at arm's length as he stammered to the other soldier, "This isn't a man! This is my girl. She dressed like a boy because she was trying to join up."

"Uh-huh," his grinning tent-mate said.

"Schmidt! It's true! Frankie, tell him you're a girl."

Frankie whirled around and, hands on hips faced the other soldier. "I'm a girl!"

"If you say so.

"I do! I'm with the laundresses."

Schmidt laughed. "Uh-huh."

Her face flushed red. "Oh, go ask Bill Crenshaw!"

The soldier laughed and walked away.

"Boy," Patrick breathed, "if he tells the sergeant about this, I'll be out on my ear."

"Oh, never mind him, Pat. Bill Crenshaw'll set him straight."

Patrick frowned. "How do you know Bill?"

Frankie smiled beguilingly. "Can't I talk to another boy?"

"No. I mean, yes. I mean... Frankie, what are you doing? You can't stay here! This is the army. No girls allowed."

"That's where you're wrong," she replied, putting her arms around him once more and pressing her cheek to his chest. She had never seen him with his shirt off. He had a little hair on his chest, but his skin was smooth. And he had nice muscles and he was so tall. She felt safe in his arms. "Girls *are* allowed, Pat."

"Since when?"

"Ever since they got laundresses, which Becky says is ever since the American Revolution. Company B's washer women needed an extra hand, so Becky took me to the Quartermaster, and I got signed up." She gazed into his eyes. "Pat, why're you washing your own clothes?"

"I'm a private, you silly goose. I can't afford to pay for a laundress. And *you* can't be a washer woman. Your mother'd never permit it."

"She would!"

"No, she wouldn't."

"Yes, she would." Then Frankie blurted something that came completely unbidden from the back part of her mind: "If we got married, she'd permit it." She immediately regretted her words. What was she doing? She wasn't sure she wanted to get married yet. Why did she say that?

Patrick's response was predictable. "*Married?*"

She was up to her ears now, so Frankie decided to make the best of it. Pulling herself up to her full height, which wasn't very much at all, she lifted her chin and said, "Yes, married! If I was your wife, Mama couldn't say anything at all."

"Frances Blaine!" Patrick let go of her.

Her heart sank as she watched him pace across the grass. Things were not going at all the way she thought they would.

He whirled back around to look at her. "Have you gone completely mad?"

"No! It's the only way we can – "

"Frankie!" Patrick marched back and stood in front of her. "There's no way you can do this. You're only sixteen years old. Your mother and Eli would have the marriage annulled and you'd be hauled back to Blaineton faster than you could blink your eyes. Besides, I don't want any wife of mine marching miles and miles and getting anywhere near a battle."

Stubbornly jutting her chin, Frankie countered, "Oh, but it's all right for you to do it, isn't it?"

"Yes, it is all right. I'm a man! I believe in the Union and I'm willing to fight for New Jersey. Frankie, please understand. I don't want to be in a battle. I don't want to get injured and I sure as hell don't want to die, but this is something I have to do." He stopped and took a breath. "And, honey," now he gently put a hand on her shoulder, "if we got married it probably wouldn't be too long before you'd be having a baby."

"A baby?" Her green eyes flew wide open.

"I wouldn't want you following the regiment in that condition."

"But maybe I wouldn't have a baby," she protested.

"Now, Frankie, you know it would happen eventually."

67

"No, it wouldn't." She squared her shoulders. "We wouldn't have to have a baby if we didn't... *you know*."

Patrick threw his hands in the air at this. "Frankie! There is no way on God's green earth that I'm gonna marry you and *not* do what married people do with each other!"

Everything was crumbling around her. Patrick was able to dispute every single thing she had offered up. It was clear he didn't want her to go with him.

A huge tear of frustration seeped from Frankie's left eye and rolled down her cheek.

"Oh, honey..." Patrick pulled a handkerchief out of his pocket. "Don't cry."

"I don't want you to die..." She covered her face with the hankie.

"And I don't *want* to die." He gathered her up in his arms again and kissed the top of her head. "Listen, I've got some news that might help. The other day the Regimental Surgeon put out a call for men who had some experience in medicine. I applied and was accepted to be part of an ambulance crew."

She looked up at him. "What's an ambulance?"

"It's a wagon we use to bring the wounded to the field hospital. Every ambulance has a driver and two men. Besides getting the men onto the wagon, I'll be binding wounds to stop bleeding and splinting broken bones if necessary."

"But you'll still be in the middle of the fighting."

"Honey, I'll be in the middle of the fighting no matter what. I'm only a private. But I promise to be careful. And I've been told that the other side won't shoot at us if they see the ambulance."

"What if you aren't by the ambulance? They'd shoot at you then."

"How about if I hang on to the side?"

"Now you're just being silly," Frankie huffed. Then her eyes grew wide. "Oh, Pat, I feel terrible!"

"What's wrong now?"

"Why did I ever do this? I left everything I own at home. I even forgot to bring my Bible with me! Everything keeps going wrong, but I can't go home anymore. Not after what I've done."

He sighed. "You're wrong, Frankie. Of course, you can go home. Your mother loves you. She'll forgive you."

"And then she'll punish me."

He chuckled. "Yeah, well, you kind of deserve it, don't you think?"

Frankie sighed. "Yes. But Papa! He'll probably lock me in my room 'til I'm an old maid!"

Patrick guffawed. "Somehow I think after he's done yelling, he'll forgive you, too."

"I suppose," Frankie admitted.

"No supposing about it. Remember the story of the Prodigal Son? It'll be the same thing with you. Your mother'll run to you the minute you walk up to the house."

She nodded contritely.

"Look, do you really want to help me?"

"You know I do, Pat."

"Then write to me. Write every single day. Even a few lines'll give me something to keep my spirits up." He took a breath. "Now, let me put a shirt on and we'll go see how we can get you home."

#

Maggie and Eli arrived at Camp Fair Oaks right on the dot of eight. The entrance to the camp presented them with a field full of rectangular tents with the sea of Sibley and wall tents beyond.

"Let's check with the recruitment tents first," Eli suggested.

Maggie's eyes swept over the line. "I imagine she went to the Company B tent, don't you?"

"That would be logical." Eli pointed his cane at the tent in question. "Shall we?"

When the couple stepped into stuffy air of the shelter, they found a young man sitting behind the enlistment desk. Having learned to read uniforms and insignia, Eli said to him, "Good morning, Lieutenant. I see Captain Burt is not here."

The first lieutenant rose. "Correct, sir. I am on duty." He hesitated. "Excuse me, but you seem to be older and..." He nodded at the cane in Eli's hand. "You carry a walking stick, and obviously not for ornamental purposes."

Eli smiled easily. "You're correct. I'm not recruitment material. We're looking for someone who may have enlisted."

"Would you give me his name?"

"It might be Frank Blaine."

The lieutenant raised an eyebrow. "Might be?"

Eli took a breath. "Brace yourself, here comes the story. We're here because my stepdaughter ran away yesterday and we were told that she had cut her hair, put on men's clothing, and wanted to join the army to be with her beau."

The lieutenant chuckled. "Again?"

"What do you mean *again*?"

"Believe it or not, sir, that has happened a few times."

"Has it?" Maggie asked with a trace of concern.

"Don't worry, ma'am. Most girls are discovered and safely returned to their families." He took a piece of paper from a drawer and dipped a pen in his ink well. "What's her name? – I mean, her *real* name?"

"Frances," Maggie said. "Frances Blaine. She's short, slim, and has red hair and green eyes."

The young man wrote the details down. "I'll send a search party to find her. If you can give me an address where you're staying –"

"Well, will you look who's here," a familiar voice behind them said.

Maggie and Eli turned to find Patrick and Frankie standing by the tent's flap.

Before anyone could move, Patrick added, "Frankie and I thought we'd come over to see what could be done about getting her home, but it looks like we don't have to do that now."

Coming out of his surprise, Eli blurted, "Frances Deborah Blaine! Do you have any idea how worried we've been? Your mother was tossing and turning all night! Both of us are exhausted."

Even before he had finished the sentence, Maggie was sweeping across the room and gathering her daughter up. "Oh, my dear child! Why would you ever do such a thing?"

Frankie melted at her mother's words. "I'm sorry, Mama. I just wanted to help the Union and I wanted to be with Patrick."

Patrick and Eli shared an eye roll. The lieutenant made note of it and chuckled. He had been privy to similar scenes a few times.

Maggie released her daughter to peer into Frankie's runny eyes. "My dear, there are some things over which we have no control and which we can't make better. And sometimes trying to do so only makes them worse." She brought a hankie out of her reticule and gave it to Frankie, who mopped her face.

"I know," her daughter sniffed. "I guess I just had to learn that for myself."

"Don't worry." Maggie smiled. "As I recall I had to learn a few lessons like that myself."

Avoiding her mother's gaze now, Frankie stoically muttered. "I suppose I'll have a punishment now." She was embarrassed, feeling foolish, and wishing she was home with everything back to normal. But that wasn't possible.

"Oh, you *will* have a punishment," Eli sternly replied. But a raised eyebrow from Maggie made him add, "Your mother, of course, will determine what that will be."

When Patrick chuckled, the older man glared at him. "And as for you..."

Patrick frowned. "And as for me, what?"

"Let's just say I hope there isn't a reason for me to beat you around the head with my cane."

The younger man exploded. "Oh, for crying out loud, Eli! Will you stop giving me that jo-fired bunk? What do you take me for?"

Eli maintained his composure. "I take you for a gentleman. Am I correct?"

"Would I be shouting like a madman if I weren't?" Patrick snapped.

Satisfied that Frankie's purity was still intact, Eli smirked. "Good. As you were, Private."

The first lieutenant chortled. "Well! Looks to me like things have turned out for the best."

"Yes, sir," Eli said. "It has. And I thank you for your help. We'll be on our way now."

As they exited the tent, Maggie took her daughter's arm and walked her away from the men so they could speak privately. "I'm so glad you're safe."

"I didn't mean to make you worry."

"But you did, Frances. I was terribly worried."

Frankie stared at her feet. "I know. I'm sorry."

"Are you ready to go home now?"

Frankie nodded.

Maggie gave her a hug. "Fine! We'll pick up our things at Pleasant Rest before we leave. I have a skirt, petticoat, and a waist for you to wear home."

Frankie hesitated. "Must I, Mama? I mean, I know I look like a boy right now, but may I change my clothes once we get home? I don't care what I look like. I don't even care what people think."

Rather than scolding her daughter and demanding that she wear a dress, Maggie said, "I see. Well, then you are stronger than most people if you don't care what others think. So, I am content to return home with my daughter dressed like a boy." She placed a hand lovingly on Frankie's cheek. "I know it doesn't matter what people think as long as you're doing the right thing."

"Do you think being dressed like a boy is the right thing for me to do?"

"Well," Maggie allowed, "I think it is after what you have been through. You need time to think about your experiences here. If staying in boys' clothing gives you that opportunity then it is the right thing to do."

The two strolled to a tree where they stood shaded by its leaves. Frankie took her mother's hand. "Mama, I finally know I'm too young to go off on my own. It's all because I met a friend here. Her name's Rosa. She's a laundress because she has no one left in the world but her brother. He works as a blacksmith for the regiment. She was willing to leave her hometown and travel with the soldiers, so she could be with him because both her parents are dead, and she has no other family."

"She sounds like a remarkable young woman," Maggie said. "I'd like to meet her."

"I'll take you to her. She must be the bravest person I've ever met. I saw what her life is like with the laundresses and it takes a lot of courage and strength. And, Mama, I'm just not ready for that – at least not for the time being. Going back to Blaineton will give me time to think about what I want to do with my life and to talk with you and Liddy and the others. If I stay at Suds Row I won't be able to talk to the people I love, let alone be with them."

"I'm glad you feel that way."

Frankie hugged her mother. "I'm so proud that you help Papa edit the *Gazette*, Mama. And I'm thankful that you let me try things out and that you encourage Liddy in her study of medicine and that you love everyone, regardless of who they are. You're the kind of woman I want to be. Even if I don't do exactly what you do, I want to be like you." Her eyes lit up. "You wouldn't believe what women are doing here at Camp Fair Oaks! Do you know they work as laundresses, nurses, and cooks?" She lowered her voice. "And, Mama, there even are woman soldiers here. I met one!"

Maggie lifted her eyebrows. "And no one has noticed?"

Frankie giggled. "No! As long as she wears trousers, no one notices at all."

Maggie chuckled. "I can't imagine such a thing!" She took a deep breath. "Well, I suppose we need to tell your head laundress that you'll be leaving your job."

Frankie's stomach clenched at the thought of facing blunt, intimidating Becky. Just the same, her mother was right. She simply couldn't disappear. As Eli might say, she needed to take her medicine.

So, Frankie screwed up her courage and escorted her mother, stepfather, and Patrick to Suds Row. On the way, she told them all about the laundresses, especially Rosa.

When they arrived, they found Becky, Rosa, and Lily scrubbing, rubbing, and mending the day's laundry. Frankie called out a greeting.

All three lifted their heads and stared at her in annoyance, which made Frankie blush. They needed all hands to get the work done and she had been absent for a long time, which had left them to handle it the whole load. That was irresponsible of her. Frankie knew for sure that she wasn't mature enough to go out on her own.

Feeling as if her feet were mired in molasses, she dragged herself over and stood anxiously before Becky.

"And where have *you* been?" Becky demanded.

"I found Patrick."

"And who are these other people?"

"My mother, Mrs. Smith, and my stepfather, Mr. Smith, and my beau, Private McCoy." She paused for a second and then forged on. "I know you've just hired me as a laundress, Becky, but I'm not ready for this life. And, as you can see, my mother has found me. I want to return home with her and my stepfather."

Becky frowned, but there wasn't a trace of anger in her reply. "Yeah. I kind of figured that would happen."

Embarrassed, Frankie quickly introduced the two groups and prayed that she would not have to own up to any other mistakes that day.

"Mm," Lily murmured. "Frankie, I see why you ran off to be with your private..."

A white-hot rush of jealousy hit her, and Frankie wanted to tell Lily to keep her hands off her beau. However, she knew that only would get her in more trouble. Then she realized that Pat wasn't even giving Lily a second look. Pleased, she smiled broadly.

"Thank you for taking my daughter in, Becky," Maggie was saying. "I'm sorry to have to take her away. But she is... well... rather inexperienced."

"Yeah." Becky chuckled. "Yeah. Just like a lamb. She's a hard worker, though. I'm gonna miss that. But she's doing the right thing. You're raising a good girl."

Frankie rolled her eyes and Patrick gave her a little nudge on the arm. When Frankie looked up at him, he grinned and gave her a wink.

"Now, then, Rosa..." Maggie said.

The dark young woman said, "Yes'm?"

"I want to thank you for befriending my daughter. She told me a little about you and I want to invite you to come live with us in Blaineton if you'd like."

"Oh, ma'am, that's real kind." Rosa stood up. "But my brother's a blacksmith with the regiment and I won't leave him."

"I thought that might be your answer. However, if you ever need anything, please come and see me. I am Mrs. Margaret Smith. I own the Second Street Boarding House on the town square."

"Thank you, ma'am. I'll do that."

"Tell me, are you able to read?"

Rosa nodded.

"Excellent." Maggie turned to her husband. "Mr. Smith, do you have paper and pencil?"

Eli chuckled. "I should hope so. I'm a newspaperman." Upon fishing a small notebook and a stubby pencil from his jacket pocket, he handed them to his wife.

Maggie wrote her information on a page, tore it out, and gave it to the girl. "This is my name and where we live. Keep it with you and know that you're welcome at any time for any reason."

"Hey, Mrs. Smith," Becky joked, "don't you go taking all my laundresses!"

Maggie laughed. "Perish the thought! It is bad enough I'm taking my daughter from you. Allow me to extend my invitation to you and Lily, as well. If any of you need help or a place to stay after the war, please do not hesitate to come to Blaineton and seek me out. This is a sincere invitation. You *will* be welcome."

"That's very kind of you," Becky said, and she meant it.

Frankie felt a little ping of pride in her heart, for the first and foremost thing about her mother was that she was always kind to everyone she met. *Someday,* she decided, *I'm going to be just like her.*

#

Frankie and Patrick were sitting on rough-hewn benches near the camp's entrance. Patrick did not have to go on duty for another few hours, so the two were spending this precious time enjoying the morning air together, while Eli and Maggie were visiting with Edgar.

The two young people sat in silence for a few minutes and then Frankie said, "I'm sorry for all the trouble I caused."

"Aw, it's fine." Patrick waved it off. "Heck, I know you. Nothing surprises me anymore."

She glanced impishly at him. "Nothing, huh?"

He chuckled. "Well, maybe not *nothing.*"

"Are we still courting?"

"Of course. After all the trouble you caused, I'm invested."

She laughed.

As they sat shaded from the sun by the leaves of the old oak tree, Patrick took her hand. Smiling with relief, Frankie rested her head on his shoulder.

"Listen," he said after a few minutes. "Once I know when the regiment's leaving, I'll send a telegram. I'd like it if you, your mother, Eli, and... well, everybody could say goodbye."

Frankie's eyes glistened with tears. "We'll be there, Pat. Don't worry."

Patrick's eyes welled up, too. "Thanks. It would mean a lot."

She wrapped her arms around him and the two hugged.

"I love you, Pat," she whispered against his neck.

"I love you, too."

"Be careful."

"I will."

"I'll write every day. I promise."

"And I'll try to stay safe."

When she could hold it back no longer, Frankie blurted, "Come back to me, please, Patrick!"

He took her chin and gazed into her elfin face. "You know I will. Frances." And he kissed her. And it lasted much more than a second.

#

True to his word, Patrick sent a wire to the boarding house, telling them that the regiment had been ordered to depart on August 29. They would be boarding the train in Flemington and making a brief stop in Lambertville before moving on.

The boarding house family once again checked their kitchen pin money. Unfortunately, the trip to Flemington had badly depleted it. However, the other residents pooled their resources and raised enough for Eli, Maggie, Lydia, and Frankie to travel to Lambertville and back. Their plan made, the four left on the early train and arrived at their destination before 9:00.

As they got off the cars, they found the depot alive with activity. People were bringing tables outside, arranging them, and covering them with tablecloths. Everywhere bunting and flags were being hung. When the family asked what was going on, a woman excitedly explained that the town wanted to welcome the Fifteenth New Jersey Volunteers and that the ladies of Lambertville were going to provide a lunch for the soldiers.

The Smith family excitedly joined in the preparations. At one point, Maggie and her daughters repaired to Lambert's Inn where they and the women of the town made sandwiches. Eli stayed at the station and continued to assist with the decorations and take notes for an article in the *Gazette.*

Around 11:00 a.m. members of the town's band arrived and set up at one end of the platform, while people began sauntering onto the depot's platform. There were men in tall top hats. Women, dressed in hoop skirts and holding parasols over their heads, conversed animatedly as children darted everywhere.

A great cheer arose from the crowd at the first sign of smoke from the approaching steam engine and the blast of its horn. As the train chugged its way toward the depot, the band struck up a song that was taking the nation by storm: "The Battle Cry of Freedom" by George F. Root. It had been printed a little over a month earlier, but everyone seemed to have the sheet music or at least know the chorus and tune. The crowd sang lustily as they waved flags and handkerchiefs.

Yes, we'll rally round the flag, boys, we'll rally once again,
Shouting the battle cry of freedom,
We will rally from the hillside, we'll gather from the plain,
Shouting the battle cry of freedom!

The Union forever! Hurrah, boys, hurrah!
Down with the traitors, up with the stars;
While we rally round the flag, boys, rally once again,
Shouting the battle cry of freedom!

Spewing steam and cinders, the train groaned to a stop. Soldiers were hanging out the windows and waving at the crowd. Frankie and Lydia hurriedly grabbed a plate of sandwiches each and pushed their way through the crush of bodies as they searched for the faces of their loved ones. Many other women were the same thing, and they had to struggle through a mass of crinolines and parasols.

While they were doing this, Frankie caught sight of a familiar face peering out a window. She abruptly stopped and called out, "Bill! Bill Crenshaw!"

The female soldier looked down at her, hesitated, and then grinned broadly. "Why, is that Frankie?"

"Yes!"

"You look different."

Frankie laughed. "It's the dress. But I've still got the short hair."

"So, you do, girl. So, you do."

A lump suddenly formed in Frankie's throat. She realized that Bill was going to face danger just like all the other soldiers. "Oh, Bill," she cried, "do be careful!"

"I'll try my best."

"Best of luck."

Bill pursed her lips as if trying to stifle the strong emotion Frankie knew she must be feeling.

"And God bless you, Bill."

The young woman nodded solemnly. "Thank you, Frankie. God bless you, too."

Eyes teary, Frankie turned and caught up to Lydia, who gazed curiously at her and asked, "Who was that?"

"Someone I met at the camp." She took a breath. "Liddy, that soldier is a girl."

Lydia's brown eyes widened. "Indeed? Well!" She gathered her thoughts. "How brave of her to do that. I'll keep her in my prayers."

"Me, too," Frankie said.

At last the sisters found their young men. Patrick and Edgar were in the second to last car. Shouting greetings, the young women passed the food up to them. The two soldiers took what they needed and handed the plates to the others in their car.

"Goodbye, darling!" Edgar shouted over the din and leaned precariously out the window. Lydia stood on her toes and lifted her head to meet his lips as her hands clung to his arms in a bid to keep her balance.

Frankie enviously watched them kiss and rued the fact that she wasn't tall like Lydia. Worse yet, she knew Patrick couldn't lean far enough out the window to kiss her without falling on his head. But she was unwilling to let her last moments with Pat pass, so she reached up to her beau. Holding his hand or even simply touching him would have to suffice.

It took her by surprise then when Patrick seized her upper arms and lifted her right off her feet. In the next second, they were face to face. When Frankie met his lips, they shared the most uncomfortable, yet most passionate kiss in all her young life.

"Be careful, Pat," she cried when their lips parted. "Oh, please be careful!"

"I will! I will, my dear!"

And they kissed again.

All the while, soldiers were being fed through the train windows and given glasses filled with lemonade. They quickly devoured the food, downed the drink, and began returning the glasses and plates.

Before Frankie knew it, everything was over, and the conductor was calling all aboard.

When the train lurched forward, Frankie and Lydia stepped back from the moving vehicle and followed Patrick and Edgar's car down the platform until they could go no further. So, they stood there waving until all the cars were out of sight.

"We must be strong," a red-eyed Lydia said, as the last puff of smoke disappeared. "We have to do it for them."

Frankie sniffed her tears in. "It still isn't fair that we have to stay at home."

Lydia gave her a tender smile. "Maybe someday that'll change. But right now, I know one thing."

"What's that?"

"If they do change, we'll have a whole new set of troubles." She slipped an arm around her sister's waist. "Come on."

As they moved through the throng of people experiencing similar feelings, they heard sobs, prayers, and expressions of love. When the Blaine sisters finally located their mother and stepfather, they were taken aback to find Maggie weeping against Eli's shoulder. As they drew closer, they saw that Eli, too, was shedding tears. Frankie impulsively threw her arms around both parents and wept with them. Lydia joined her.

"Oh, my dears," a surprised Maggie said. "I'm afraid I'm making a spectacle. I'm sorry."

"Well, I'm not sorry," Eli sniffed. "I hate war."

When the girls broke the embrace, Eli searched his pockets for a handkerchief, pulled off his eyeglasses, and wiped his face. Maggie produced her hankie and dabbed her wet eyes.

"Why are *you* crying, Mama?" Frankie asked.

Maggie sighed. "It's that they're all so young and..." She quickly put a hand on each daughter's face. "...and *you're* so young. Yet, here you are, forced into maturity before you're ready."

Frankie straightened her spine. "Don't worry, Mama. We're strong." She took Lydia's hand. "We're women. We can do anything."

As Frankie glanced around the platform, she found that after all the excitement, the place seemed tired and a bit ramshackle.

She smiled at her family. "Come on. It looks like it's time to clean up."

Glossary

Adventuress – Prostitute.

Bodice – The part of a dress that covers the chest. Dresses didn't have pockets, so Frankie would have hidden her handkerchief down her bodice (especially since it was summer, and she wasn't wearing long sleeves).

Cooling board – A board on which a corpse was placed. It was used in preparing the body for the funeral and for the viewing. Ice was placed beneath the board to slow the process of decomposition. Usually, the container for the ice and the board were disguised with fabric so the deceased looked as if he or she were lying on a bed.

Drawers – Underpants with legs.

Johnnies – Slang term for Confederate soldiers, a short form of "Johnny Reb (Rebel)."

Larder – A cool place where food can be stored.

Minié ball – A cylindrical bullet with a hollow base. The minié bullet expanded when fired. It was accurate and lethal over long distances and could do terrible damage to those it hit.

Necessary – Referring to "the necessary" is a polite way of saying "outhouse."

Negro – This term has a long history. While frowned upon today, it was preferred when referring to Black people in the mid-1900s. However, in the 1860s, it also was used to describe slaves. This is why Rosa, a free person of color, takes such exception when McCarthy uses the term to describe her.

Painted women and hussies – Derogatory terms for women who engaged in activities outside the usual moral values of the culture. Th e phrase was also used when referring to prostitutes or sexually promiscuous women. "Painted women" wore makeup to attract men. Impudent or immoral females were called "hussies."

Scrapple – A meatloaf made of scraps of ground meat (often pork) mixed with broth, cornmeal, and spices, and served in slices. It is a Pennsylvania Dutch food but is common throughout eastern Pennsylvania. The cook at Camp Fair Oaks was probably looking for a way to stretch her food budget!

Shut you pan and *saw your timber* – slang for "shut up and go away."

Swab - Strips of cloth tied to a stick and used for cleaning dishes.

Underground Railroad line – a secret web of people who opened their homes, barns, and other buildings to self-emancipating people. People working the Underground Railroad often escorted escaping slaves to the next stop on the route. The Underground Railroad was designed to move people to Mexico or to northern destinations such as New York City, Boston, and Canada.

Wash boiler – A large metal container used for boiling clothes that could also be used for boiling water for other occasions, such as bathing and washing dishes.

Annotated Bibliography

Writing historical fiction is a strange activity. It requires an author to do the usual business of character development, plotting, themes, and more but has an additional aspect: doing research so the story is accurate to its time and place.

Below is a list the references I used in writing this story and a bit of commentary.

Civil War Laundresses

Leverette, Mary Marlowe. "Laundry During the Civil War - The Laundress." *The Spruce.* 09 07, 2016. https://www.thespruce.com/laundry-during-the-civil-war-laundress-2146296 (accessed June 03, 2017).

Mescher, Virginia. "Virginia's Veranda." *Ragged Soldier.* 2013. http://www.raggedsoldier.com/final_laundry_vv.pdf (accessed April 2017).

When I started to write about Frankie's adventure at Camp Fair Oaks, I had no clear idea what laundresses did and bought into the idea that female "camp followers" primarily were prostitutes. How wrong I was! Both Leverette and Mescher make it clear that all laundresses were not women of ill repute. In fact, Mescher notes that the army wanted women of good character as washerwomen, although Leverette suggests that some laundresses most likely engaged in sexual activities with the soldiers and/or were husband-hunters like Lily. On the other hand, most probably were like Rosa and Becky, who followed the men in their lives.

Food and Housework

Beecher, Catharine E. *A Treatise on Domestic Economy, for the Use of Young Ladies at Home and at School.* New York: Harper & Brothers, 1845.
—. *Miss Beecher's Domestic Receipt Book: Designed as a Supplement to Her Treatise on Domestic Economy.* New Year: Harper & Brothers, 1846.

I used Beecher's *Treatise* for information regarding mid-nineteenth-century tools and processes that people might have used to wash dishes. Remarkably, the items washed first, middle, and last in those days was the same process I learned for washing up in the pre-dishwasher days of my youth! The rest of the book is a fascinating glimpse into women's domestic lives and what Beecher thought and advised her readers to adopt (i.e., she hated corsets and promoted exercise). I turned to Beecher's *Domestic Receipt Book* to research the foods my characters might eat. Foodies might find this book a fun read and even might dare to make a few of dishes, although with adjustments for contemporary tastes.

Female Soldiers

"Female Soldiers in the Civil War." *Civil War.org.* n.d. https://www.civilwar.org/learn/articles/femalesoldierscivilwar (accessed June 06, 2017).

Wakeman, Sarah Rosetta. *An Uncommon Soldier: The Civil War Letters of Sarah Rosetta Wakeman, alias Pvt. Lyons Wakeman, 153rd Regiment, New York State Volunteers, 1862-1864.* Edited by Lauren Cook Burgess. New York: Oxford University Press, 1995.

There are a number of books and articles available that deal with women passing as men among the ranks of Civil War soldiers. My main sources for this story about female soldiers were the articles found in the Civil War Trust website (www.civilwar.org) and Lauren Cook Burgess' curation of Sarah Rosetta Wakeman's letters. These gave me insight into the life of female soldiers, who they were, and why they fought. The Civil War Trust's web page, "Female Soldiers in the Civil War" notes that while women's participation in the military was secretive and thus makes hard numbers impossible to obtain, "conservative estimates of female soldiers in the Civil War put the number [of women soldiers] somewhere between 400 and 750." Interestingly, women joined up for many of the same reasons as men: patriotism, pay, the desire for adventure, and more. They also enlisted if a loved one, such as a husband, was in the service.

We may wonder why females in the ranks were not more readily discovered. Incredible as it seems today, several reasons have been suggested. 1) Victorian modesty dictated that things such as bathing and attending to nature's call often were done in private, thus many soldiers would be modest. 2) Soldiers tended to sleep in their clothing. 3) Physical examinations were cursory. As long as the prospective soldier did not present with obvious signs of illness, he was deemed healthy and there was no need for him to remove his clothing. 4) Uniforms were heavy and bulky. 5) The general lack of military experience among men meant that female soldiers experienced the same learning curve as the men and did not stand out among the ranks. 6) Gender in the nineteenth century was associated with the clothing one wore. Succinctly put, if a woman donned men's clothing, she was perceived to be a man, at least by other men. For, despite their masquerade, Lauren Cook Burgess writes in her Introduction to *An Uncommon Soldier* that other women did seem to be able to recognize their same-sex comrades. She postulates that this may be because women could see beyond the façade of dress. Thus, in *The Enlistment*, Bill Crenshaw is able to recognize Frankie, even though Maggie's daughter is dressed as a boy.

My character Bill Crenshaw has her roots in Union soldier Sarah Rosetta Wakeman. Like Wakeman, Bill left a household comprised of numerous mouths to feed and an indebted father. Women were paid low wages and had limited job opportunities, so when Bill and Wakeman saw that they could earn more money as a soldier and realized it would help them provide additional income for their families, they enlisted.

The Fifteenth New Jersey Volunteers

Bilby, Joseph G. *Three Rousing Cheers: A History of the Fifteenth New Jersey from Flemington to Appomattox*. Hightstown, NJ: Longstreet House, 1993.

Haines, Alanson A. *History of the Fifteenth Regiment New Jersey Volunteers*. New York: Jenkins & Thomas, Printers, 1883.

One of the biggest frustrations in writing this novella was the lack of specific information on the Fifteenth New Jersey Volunteers. I was excited to discover not one, but two books on the subject. The work by Haines is a first-person memoir published 23 years after the end of the Civil War. The other by Joseph Bilby is a contemporary history of the regiment. They provided details about the regiment's founding, camp activities, and the regiment's reception in Lambertville as the soldiers left for the war. And imagine my surprise when, upon receipt of the Bilby book, I discovered that it had been signed by the author. It may not be technically a collector's item, but I was thrilled to see the author's signature. Those interested in military history in general and New Jersey military history during the Civil War might find these two books a worthy addition to a collection. Although the Bilby book is out of print, one can still find copies for sale on the internet. The Haines book, on the other hand, has been reprinted and is readily available for purchase.

Railroad Information

Travelers' Official Railway Guide for the Railways (June 1870). Central Pacific Railroad Photographic History Museum. June 1870. http://cprr.org/Museum/Travellers_Guide_6-1870.html (accessed June 22, 2017).

Another challenge in writing *The Enlistment* was learning train routes and schedules. When I realized that I was going to have to coordinate the train departures and arrivals of my characters, I had no idea where to look and thought I was going to have to make something up. In other words, I was going to have to put the "fiction" into "historical fiction." But then my partner and train fan Dan Bush suggested I consult something called *The Travelers' Official Railway Guide for the Railways*. It was a book put out in the nineteenth through twentieth centuries either yearly or bi-annually. The *Railway Guide* provided travelers and train stations with timetables for all railroads in North America as well as other information. While writing THE ENLISTMENT, I was unable to find a guide earlier than 1870. Apparently, that was the first year it was published under that name. I did find another guide under another name, but since I had already gone into great detail about the train schedules in the story, I decided to use the 1870 schedules. After all, I'm not writing a detailed text on the history of train schedules in Warren and Hunterdon Counties, New Jersey. I'm writing historical *fiction*.

About the Author

As founder and CEO of Squeaking Pips Press (2007), Janet wears many hats: author, editor, designer, and encourager of new authors. Although born in Albany, New York, Janet spent most of her childhood and the bulk of her teen years in Parsippany, NJ. She attended Seton Hall University (South Orange, NJ) where she received a B.A. degree in Asian Studies. Years later she attended Drew University and received a Master of Divinity degree and a Ph.D. in North American Religion and Culture. Janet has worked as an adjunct professor over the course of six years at two universities and taught interdisciplinary studies and history. In addition, she has had a long tenure serving the United Methodist Church. At 25 years and counting, she has served six congregations, working predominantly in the area of spiritual formation and ministries with children and youth. She has been with her current congregation since 2008.

Through Squeaking Pips, Janet has published five novels and several short stories. The majority are part of the Saint Maggie Series and are set in Civil War era America. The novels - SAINT MAGGIE, WALK BY FAITH, A TIME TO HEAL, and SEEING THE ELEPHANT – follow the adventures of Maggie, her husband Eli, and their unconventional family as they face the challenges of the 1860s.

In addition, Janet has written two short stories based on the Saint Maggie series, "The Christmas Eve Visitor" and "The Dundee Cake," and plans to write a series of longer works that feature Maggie's daughters. Janet also has adapted "The Christmas Eve Visitor" as a play, which she hopes to produce someday.

Janet's other work is the contemporary romance, HEART SOUL & ROCK'N'ROLL, which began as a film script, became a novel and is now a film script again. She hopes to write a sequel to the book.

Other Works by Janet R. Stafford

Historical Fiction
A woman of faith, her free-thinking husband, and their un-conventional family struggle to survive and thrive in 1860s America.

Saint Maggie (2011)
Maggie Blaine, a widow with two teenage daughters, runs a rooming house smack dab on the town square. In 1860 this makes her a social out-cast. Boarding houses are only semi-respectable and hers has a collection of eclectic boarders – an aging writer, an undertaker's apprentice, a strug-gling young lawyer, and an old Irishman. In addition, she is friends with Emily and Nate, the Black couple with whom she shares her home, life, and chores. Given all that, it is fortunate that the town doesn't know Maggie, Nate, Emily, and Eli Smith (the free-thinking editor of the weekly newspaper) are also station masters in the Underground Railroad. When Maggie sud-denly is asked to house the new Methodist minister, handsome, gifted Jeremiah Madison, she hopes he will revive the little church she attends as well as provide her boarding house with a bit of badly-needed respectability. But Jeremiah comes with secrets that challenge her determination to love everyone. As she, her family, and town reel from a series of shocking events, the compassionate Maggie searches for truth and forgiveness. (Based on a historical event.) 2012 B.R.A.G. Medallion™ Honoree

Walk by Faith (2013)
It is the middle of the Civil War and things have gotten ugly in Blainet-on, New Jersey. Maggie never thought the Second Street boarding house would be burned to the ground. Nor did she consider that her husband Eli's print shop, home to *The Gazette* penny weekly, would suffer the same fate, and that friend Nate Johnson would be beaten because of his race. But the abolitionist sympathies of Maggie and those in her boarding house have made them a target for Copperhead forces. When the violence gets worse, Eli's sisters offer them a chance to escape and help them aid runaway slaves escape the war at the old Smith home in Gettysburg, Pennsylvania. The family undertakes the move, hoping to find some badly-needed peace. While newspaperman Eli and reporter/photographer Chester Carson are off cover-ing the war, Eli's absence creates a wedge between himself and Maggie. Starting over in a new place also does not come easy for those left in Gettys-burg. They need to find new sources of income and must adjust to the bustling Pennsylvania town. Just as they start to feel as if they are settling in, new and disturbing rumors start to fly about an impending invasion by the Confederate army.

A Time to Heal (2014)

Set in the months immediately after the Battle of Gettysburg, A TIME TO HEAL continues the story of Maggie and Eli Smith and their unconventional family. Maggie's friends and daughters have remained in Gettysburg to care for a houseful of wounded soldiers. Meanwhile, Maggie and Emily, having suffered terrible trauma during the battle, have moved with their husbands to a more peaceful location. Everyone is hoping and praying for healing and a return to normal life. But an act of compassion is mistaken for civil disobedience, putting the family in jeopardy once again.

The Christmas Eve Visitor (short story, 2015)

Sometimes miracles happen when you expect them least but need them most. It is Christmas Eve of 1863. As a snowstorm howls outside, Maggie and her family care for the family's three youngest children, all of whom are seriously ill. A knock at the door brings an unanticipated interruption in the form of an odd little peddler. Despite her anxiety over the children, Maggie invites the stranger in and feeds him supper, an act of kindness that has an impact on her entire family.

The Dundee Cake (short story, 2016)

A prequel to the Saint Maggie Series. It is Christmas of 1852. But Maggie Blaine is finding scant joy in the holiday. Having lost her husband nearly three years previously and her much-beloved Aunt Letty earlier that year, she struggles to maintain the boarding house and feed and care for those living in it. Finally, she hires a woman named Emily Johnson to help with the cooking and, even though Maggie is white, and Emily is Black, the two women become friends. When Emily and her husband Nate suffer a disaster, the financially-challenged Maggie searches for a way to help them.

Seeing the Elephant (2016)

"Seeing the elephant" (or "I've seen the elephant") means "now I've seen everything" or "now I've seen it all." Civil War soldiers also used the term to mean they had been in a battle. Maggie and her family have seen the elephant, too. Scarred from their experience in Gettysburg, they finally return to the safety of Blaineton, New Jersey only to find that their hometown is not the same. An insane asylum has opened on a hill north of town – and it is where Maggie's daughter Frankie finds employment, much to everyone's trepidation. To Blaineton's south, a woolen mill and army uniform factory are doing a booming business. And then there's Josiah Norton, a wealthy industrialist who is out to change the face and tenor of their little town, something that raises the curiosity of Eli Smith, the new Editor-in-Chief of the Blaineton *Register*.

Romance

Heart Soul & Rock 'N' Roll (2015)

Lins Mitchell, assistant minister at the Church of the Epiphany, has hit mid-life crisis. Recalling the joy of being in a college rock band, she says she wants to "rock one more time before I die!" To give her a change of pace, friend Patti invites her to vacation at her summer home in Point Pleasant Beach, New Jersey. There Lins meets Neil Gardner, leader of a bar band called the Grim Reapers. He is looking for a new lead singer and is first captivated by Lins' voice and later by Lins herself. But Lins is uncertain. Should she really be having a whirlwind romance with an agnostic who seems to have a messy life?

www.ingramcontent.com/pod-product-compliance
Lightning Source LLC
Chambersburg PA
CBHW020412150626
46554CB00013B/831